THE MUSIC GUIDE

to
Belgium
Luxembourg
Holland
and
Switzerland

THE MUSIC

ELAINE BRODY
CLAIRE BROOK

GUIDE to Belgium
Luxembourg
Holland
and
Switzerland

Dodd, Mead & Company
New York

1   2   3   4   5   6   7   8   9   10

Library of Congress Cataloging in Publication Data

Brody, Elaine.
  The music guide to Belgium, Luxembourg, Holland, and Switzerland.

  Includes index.
  1. Music–Belgium–Directories. 2. Music–Luxembourg–Directories. 3. Music–Netherlands–Directories. 4. Music–Switzerland–Directories. I. Brook, Claire, joint author. II. Title.

ML21.B773   780'.25'492   77-6446
ISBN 0-396-07437-5

Preface

This book, conceived in frustration, was born into a world besieged by unprecedented economic problems. It was originally planned as one mammoth volume covering eighteen European countries, but like so many grandiose projects, has fallen victim to our current recession. The result is a series of self-contained fragments—each book treating a specific country or area and each one available at a negotiable price. However, this necessary compromise has moved us far from our original intention.

How did it all start?

We both travel as much as our professional responsibilities will allow. We are both trained musicians married to men whose work requires them to spend some part of each year in Europe and we try to accompany them whenever possible. Too often, however, we have found ourselves in the right city at the wrong time or—worse still—in the right city at the right time without being aware of it until it was too late.

Often when faced with the delightful prospect of a few weeks abroad, we have been astonished at how difficult it is to acquire sufficient information to make these visits as fruitful as possible. The musical traveler has no central source of data on a multitude of questions practical, historical, or theoretical. There are those who want to be sure that if they are in Bayreuth on a Tuesday, they can visit the theater even though there is no performance; others may try for weeks to isolate the moment when the Musée d'Instruments of the Paris Conservatory receives visitors and allows them to play the instruments on display; the curious amateur may wish to locate the Brahms House in Baden-Baden, while others may have heard that there is an interesting music festival in Fishguard without being able to guess exactly where it is and when it is held. Graduate students seeking to avail themselves of the resources of the Gesellschaft der Musikfreunde in Vienna will be grateful for precise information concerning the visiting hours and credentials requirements; the opera lover enjoying a performance at La Scala would have to be aware of the proximity of La Scala Theater Museum in order to explore it during an intermission. The young scholar arriving in Rome on a two weeks' summer leave, only to find that all the libraries are closed and there is no one within miles to provide a bit of assistance, could have been forewarned had schedules been available to him. And so on and so on and so on.

The idea for the *Music Guide* came to us in recognition of the need for a handbook which could provide to the widest range of people— from the musical dilettante to the highly motivated specialist—a compendium of information of a practical nature. The idea seemed so straightforward and obvious that we could not understand why such a guide did not already exist. Once we had embarked on the project, we understood only too well; it had not already been done because it was utterly impossible!!!

But we are getting a bit ahead of ourselves. The *Guide,* once we began to classify and organize the areas for investigations, began to shape itself. Certain editorial decisions concerning the geographical limitations of this volume had to be made arbitrarily. In addition, we would not know just how to treat individual cities until enough information had been gathered to determine the extent of the musical activity and resources in each place. Questionnaires were prepared in five languages for five categories. With the invaluable cooperation of the official cultural offices in each of the eighteen countries we had decided to discuss, we amassed lists of places and people that formed the basis of a large initial mailing. So the process of information-gathering began. As the responses came in, most of our questions concerning inclusion, exclusion, format, and style were answered. The results are to be found in the volumes that follow.

Within each country, the physical, political, and musical organizations indigenous to that nation determined the ordering of the material. In some instances, a chapter consists of a series of short essays on individual cities; in others where there is only one important urban center, additional information applying to cities outside that center is provided by categories: i.e., miscellaneous opera houses and concert halls, libraries, conservatories, etc. We have taken it upon ourselves to enter the lists editorially by making evaluative judgments.

In addition to decisions of qualitative merit, we have had to take cognizance of length and usefulness. We have tried to maintain a reasonable level of consistency in approach and depth of information. Although we sent the same questionnaires to each country, the responses were incredibly uneven. In some cases information was unavailable because we received no replies and it was impossible to pursue the matter personally. In other instances one of us did the necessary legwork to ferret out answers when the official sources were uncooperative. Very often, however, we received invaluable help from many of the Music Information Centers (CeBeDeM in Brussels, Donemus in Amsterdam, the Music Information Centers of Finland and Sweden, to mention but a few) as well as from individuals whose professional affiliations enabled them to provide us with precise details in addition to general information.

Subject to geographical variations, the information we have prepared is organized under the following general headings: Opera Houses and Concert Halls; Libraries and Museums; Conservatories and Schools; Musical Landmarks; Musical Organizations; Business of Music; Miscellaneous. At the conclusion, there is a section devoted to Festivals and Competitions.

Opera Houses and Concert Halls: we have tried to include the information necessary for the reader's use in determining season, program, and hours of performances. Although we mention some churches in which concerts usually take place, we have not attempted to be overly comprehensive, since almost every church will house the odd public concert from time to time and this does not automatically qualify it as a site for musical entertainment. There has been an increasingly prevalent tendency to present concerts, opera, and chamber music in castles, courtyards, parks, and gardens. The reader is therefore advised to consult a local newspaper or concert guide, which will be indicated at the beginning of most city segments, for details of the unusual events taking place in the unexpected places.

Libraries and Museums: to facilitate practical reference to specific collections, we have attempted to give library and museum names in their original languages. We wish to acknowledge here and now our gratitude for the scholarship and generosity of Rita Benton, whose *Directory of Music Research Libraries* constituted the basic foundation of our investigations in this category. (Hence Ben. 1, 2, etc. found in our volumes refer to Dr. Benton's numbering system.) We are particularly grateful to Dr. Benton for permission to see the third volume of this important work while it was still in manuscript. For more detailed information about the institutions mentioned in this present volume, please consult her book. Where our questionnaires contained information at odds with hers, we assumed that we had the more recent data.

For the most recent and most comprehensive coverage of archives, collections, libraries, and museums, consult the cumulative index (vols. I-V, 1967–1971) of RILM (acronym for the *International Repertory of Music Literature*), an absolutely essential reference work available at most libraries.

Established in 1966 by the International Musicological Society and the International Association of Music Libraries to attempt to deal with the explosion in musicological documentation by international cooperation and modern technology, *RILM,* a quarterly publication of abstracts of books, articles, essays, reviews, dissertations, catalogues, iconographies, etc. is available in the USA through the International RILM Center, City University of New York, 33 West 42nd Street, New York 10036. European subscriptions are available from RILM Distributor for Europe, Bärenreiter Verlag Heinrich-Schütz-Allee 31–37, D-3500 Kassel-Wilhelmshöhe, West Germany.

Institutes of Musicology are to be found under different headings according to their function within the host country. In France, for example, the Institute is part of the university and is found under Schools and Conservatories. In Spain, it is a library and publishing organization and will appear under Libraries.

Schools and Conservatories: we have had to eliminate ruthlessly all but the major musical institutions in the interest of keeping this book portable. Because course offerings and degree requirements differ from country to country, we have eschewed program descriptions and instead supplied an address from which the interested reader may obtain further information. Summer courses are included in this section, except where they are clearly allied with a festival, in which case they can be located through a cross reference. A cautionary word: those planning to attend seminars or master classes in European universities should bear in mind that no housing arrangements are made by the university. The administration will supply the names of private persons who take in boarders, but these arrangements should be made well in advance of arrival. A list of organizations with special services for the English-speaking student abroad can be found in the Appendix.

Musical Landmarks: after an enthusiastic beginning, it became apparent that it would not be possible to include every commemorative plaque and graveyard that concerned a musician or musical event without rivaling the telephone directory in size. Therefore, we have usually restricted ourselves to establishments which are open to the public but do not qualify as museums. Occasionally the address of such a place seems to differ in alternate descriptions of the same place. This is invariably due to the fact that building compounds may have entrances on several streets. Where a mailing address is at variance with the public entrance, we have indicated both.

Musical organizations of international significance have been mentioned and, in some exceptional instances, described in detail. The same criteria were applied to commercial musical establishments.

The concluding section, that devoted to Festivals, Competitions, and Periodicals, brings together a body of material never before found between the covers of a single volume. Because we did not wish to build immediate obsolescence into the book, we have not supplied exact dates or typical programs for Festivals and Competitions. Instead, we have sought to give an accurate name and address to which the reader might address himself for that information. We did attempt, wherever possible, to provide descriptive as well as factual material on the more colorful festivals.

There is always a question, where co-authorship is concerned, about the division of labor in any particular project. We are sure that others have arranged their mode of cooperation in a variety of ways. Once the operational procedures had been established by mutual decision, we found it expedient and practical to divide our work on a geographical basis. Therefore, Elaine Brody supervised the research and wrote up the materials on Germany and Austria, Belgium, the Netherlands, Spain, Portugal, Switzerland, Luxembourg, and Monaco; Claire Brook did the same for Great Britain, France, Italy, and the four Scandinavian countries: Denmark, Finland, Norway, and Sweden.

The problems inherent in this kind of compendium are legion. Having to depend on the cooperation of hundreds of functionaries from secretaries to cultural ministers—disinterested at one extreme and overly zealous at the other—as well as on our own researching techniques and efforts, has resulted in somewhat uneven coverage with somewhat variable accuracy quotient. Although we have visited almost every one of the cities discussed in depth and many of those covered more cursorily, we have not attended all the festivals nor have we physically investigated all the libraries, institutes, and museums. It has been utterly impossible to check all of our sources personally. We have tried to circumvent this lapse from scholarly grace by choosing our sources as carefully as we could.

Three years after we began this Herculean task, we halted the gathering, collating, checking, writing. It would not be accurate to say that we "finished," for we are both only too aware of the fact that we have barely skimmed the surface of the material. But our manuscript had already become five times the length contracted for, and other duties called. In those three years we had the good fortune to work with a group of exceptional people—exceptional not only because of their extraordinary sense of responsibility and selfless dedication to their nation's music, but also for the care and precision with which they answered our questions. We would like to thank the following people— and to apologize to those whom we have inevitably and inadvertently overlooked: John Amis (London), Dr. R. Angermüller (Salzburg), the Comtesse de Chambure (Paris), Ulla Christiansen (New York), Hans Conradin (Zurich), Adrienne Doignies-Musters (Brussels), Ady Egleston (New York), Dr. Georg Feder (Cologne), Marna Feldt (New York), Jean and Mimi Ferrard (Brussels), Prof. Kurt von Fischer (Zurich), Claire Van Gelder (Paris and Brussels), Dr. Jörn Göres (Dusseldorf), Marlene Haag (Salzburg), Prof. Edmund Haines (New York), Ernesto Halffter (Madrid), Dr. Hilde Hellmann (Vienna), Per-Anders Hellquist (Stockholm), Maurice Huisman (Brussels), Antonio Iglesias (Madrid), Dr. Erwin Jacobi (Zurich), Jean Jenkins (London), Newell Jenkins (Giglio and New York), Prof. Rudolf Klein (Vienna), Kåre Kolberg (Oslo), Dr. Johanna Kral (Vienna), Dr. Gunnar Larsson (Stockholm), Albert Vander Linden (Brussels), Anders Lönn (Stockholm), Per Olaf Lundahl (Stockholm), René de Maeyer (Brussels), Matilde Medina y Crespo (Madrid), Per Onsum (Oslo), Dr. Alfons Ott (Munich), Pierluigi Petrobelli (Parma), Henry Pleasants (London), Andrew Porter (New York and London), Sheila Porter (New York and London), Anders Ramsay (Stockholm), Albi Rosenthal (London), Dag Schjelderup-Ebbe (Oslo),

Torben Schousboe (Copenhagen), Jarmo Sermilä (Helsinki), Sheila Solomon (London), Anna van Steenbergen (Brussels), Jean Touzelet (Paris), Edmund Tracey (London), Tatu Tuohikorpi (New York and Helsinki), Renaat Verbruggen (Antwerp), Linde Vogel (New York), William Weaver (Monte San Savino), Henry Weinberg (Florence and New York).

We would also like to acknowledge the invaluable help we received from the team of graduate students and research assistants who have supplied so much of the energy and muscle for this project. They include: Asya Berger, Louise Basbas, Lisa Mann Burke, Pamela Curzon, Hinda Keller Farber, Anne Gross, Peter Kazaras, Debbie Moskowitz, and Barbara Petersen.

And, finally, we two very liberated women would like to thank our husbands for their encouragement, patience, and touching faith that sooner or later we would emerge from behind the mountains of colored questionnaires better people for having written the *Music Guide*.

ELAINE BRODY
CLAIRE BROOK

Contents

Luxembourg   53

Holland   57

THE MUSIC GUIDE

to

Belgium
Luxembourg
Holland
and
Switzerland

Knokke

Antwerp

Bruges

Mechelen

Ghent

Louvain

Liège

Brussels

Verviers

Kortrijk

Waterloo

Tournai

Namur

Mons

Belgium

Belgium

Belgium has one of the best public relations networks of any country we have surveyed. Nevertheless, in its brochures and advertisements, surprisingly little space has been devoted to Belgium's role in the development of Western music. In retrospect, however, we can understand why.

Historically, the name Belgium rarely appears in discussions of early music. Instead, the words, Netherlands, Flanders, or the Low Countries describe the territory and the two ethnic groups—French-speaking (Walloon) and Dutch-speaking (Flemish)—that together comprise the one country. Curiously, most of the distinguished composers known as the Flemish School during the fifteenth and sixteenth centuries lived in what is now Belgium. Her musicians achieved prominence in all the major musical centers of Europe as well as in the New World.

Between 1450 and 1600, Antwerp and Brugge (the Flemish north) and Liège and Mons (the Walloon south) produced, between them, composers such as Johannes Ciconia (c. 1335–1411), Arnold de Lantins (c. 1400–?), Hugo de Lantins (before 1400–?), Hayne von Gizeghem (fl. 1457–1472), and the great master Johannes Ockeghem (1430–1495), one of the foremost innovators of his day. Jacob Obrecht (1452–1505), Heinrich Isaac (c. 1450–1517), the phenomenal Josquin des Prez (c. 1450–1521), Adrian Willaert (c. 1490–1562), Giaches de Wert (1535–1596), Nicholas Gombert (c. 1490–1556), Jacob Arcadeldt (c. 1505–1560), Clemens non Papa (c. 1510–1556), Philippe Verdelot (?–c. 1550), Philippe de Monte (1521–1603), Cipriano de Rore (1516–1565), and the world-famous Orlando di Lasso (1532–1594) were also Flemish. Many of these gentlemen traveled widely, and the names of Willaert, Lasso, and Josquin figure prominently in historical records and archives of numerous countries to the south, particularly France and Italy.

Although Belgian composers today cannot match the accomplishments of their illustrious predecessors, a long-established tradition of government support for and encouragement of cultural activities assures music a significant role in contemporary Belgian society. All year long—even during the Christmas season, when many countries have less going on than usual—Belgium offers a wide variety of events from which to choose: opera, ballet, nativity pageants, and concerts in churches, to name but a few.

Unfortunately, a serious problem confronts the cultural ministers of this state in the matter of language. Belgium is basically a bilingual country—there is a minority of German-speaking people in the east—but the individual citizens themselves are fiercely monolingual. Brussels, for example, is a French-speaking city centered in the Flemish part of the province of Brabant, the only province with no border adjoining a foreign country. Brugge—or Bruges as it is known in French—Antwerp, and Ghent are the principal Flemish cities of the north, while Liège and Mons are the French-speaking cities of the south. Most Flemings have a fair knowledge of French and often English and German; most of the French are monolingual. In the Flemish cities, however, those not speaking the host language are an uncomfortable minority, because Flemings will not speak other languages on home territory.

Nine and one half million inhabitants live in an area of 11,750 square miles. The Flemish language, very similar to Dutch, is spoken by five million Flemings; three million Walloons in the south speak French. Brussels, considered bilingual, has four-fifths of its population speaking French and one-fifth Flemish. In addition, in a small section of Belgium (near Germany), German is spoken.

Of Belgium's four universities, Liège is French, Ghent is Flemish, and Brussels and Leuven, both of which are bilingual, have each recently split into two monolingual universities. (Brussels, therefore, has two universities, while Leuven's French-speaking university has moved across the linguistic border to Ottignies.) Numerous technical and professional institutions in the country are also divided linguistically. All schools welcome foreigners, but do investigate in advance the group of your choice.

The Belgian National Radio is a very effective force in promotion and propagation of good music. Yet, when a radio tower is planned, money must be raised for two towers. Should the Flemings get one, another must be constructed for the French. In Brussels, at the theater, in the opera house or concert hall, all information—plot summaries, characters, announcements—are printed in four languages: French, Flemish, German, and English. In the classified phone book, the indices are given in the same four languages, but French and Flemish alternate each year for first and second place. In Brussels, street signs are in both French and Flemish; in some Flemish sections of the country, all signs are in Flemish.

In Brussels, a child's destiny is determined by the school to which his parents decide to send him—as early as kindergarten. If it is a French institution, he is raised French, and he will be able to teach (should he desire to do so) only in French schools. If the school is Flemish, he will speak Flemish, and will earn his living in a Flemish institution of learning. This separatism, so fundamental to the lifestyle of the citizen, is impossible for a foreigner to comprehend unless he has lived for a while in the country. The bitterness and frustration that result from this situation might almost be compared to the plight of the Blacks in America. In recent years, the situation has reversed itself. Political power today rests with the Flemish majority, and Flanders supports a far more stable economy than does the French sector of Belgium. The thriving port of Antwerp, for example, rates third among the world's seaports after New York and Rotterdam, while the Walloons (in the French part of the country) are currently closing their last coal mine—and coal for over a century has been the basis of their economy.

Belgians sometimes speak of the dual streams of cultural and artistic achievements which blend and merge with one another. Occasionally, however, confrontation is inevitable. All candid Belgians will admit it. Albert van der Linden, the curator of the library of the Royal Conservatory at Brussels, has stated that with the majority of Belgian composers "*impersonality* is the salient feature." Because of their complicated origins, Belgian musicians of the twentieth century have succumbed to a variety of influences: the German of Wagner and Strauss, followed by César Franck and his disciples (many of whom, although Belgian-born, studied and wrote in France), and, later, Debussy and Ravel. At mid-century, Stravinsky, Berg, Bartók, Hindemith, Stockhausen, and Boulez have all had their followers, but some among them stand out above the rest. Three of these are André Souris (1899-1970), Henri Pousseur (b. 1929), the first Belgian to work with electronic music, and Frederik Van Rossum (b. 1939), who recently won the Grand Prix de Rome.

Musicology in Belgium reflects the various backgrounds of its founders as well as the enormously rich assemblage of musical manuscripts, books, and instruments that were collected here. Suzanne Clercx, Robert Wangermée, Abbé Réné Lenaerts, and Albert van der Linden are Belgian names familiar to all musicologists. The Société Belge de Musicologie, organized after the war in 1946 with Charles van den Borren as its first president, publishes the *Revue Belge de Musicologie,* containing material on all branches of musicology including ethnomusicology. The late pianist, Arthur de Greef, the violinist, Arthur Grumiaux, the late conductor, André Cluytens, and the organist, Flor Peeters are Belgian performers of international reputation.

In an effort to increase the number of concert halls, a notable structure, the Palais des Beaux-Arts, was established in Brussels in 1929-30. The Concerts de Midi at Brussels, Liège, Antwerp, and Mons, where ticket costs are minimal, achieved a democratization of concert life. The establishment of the Orchestre National de Belgique in 1936, the Jeunesses Musicales in 1940, and the growth of the Concerts Populaires subsidized since 1949 by the National Ministry of Education and Culture, the recent attempts to bring the Béjart Ballet du XXe Siècle before audiences of all social classes, and, above all, the extensive efforts of the radio and recording industry have placed music in the foreground of Belgian cultural activities. The National Radio, for example, supports hundreds of public concerts and daily offers its listeners many hours of orchestral and chamber music with records from its extraordinarily comprehensive collection. Professor Robert Wangermée, a scholar with a practical side to his nature, is one of those people largely responsible for the success of these programs. He originated the idea for the monthly, *Clés pour la musique*, which is unique among the publications of radio stations, and could serve as an example for others to imitate.

One unusual feature of Belgian musical life is the practice of renting records, which has been possible since 1953, when the Discothèque Nationale was established, along with branches in many provincial cities and a Discobus that services the smaller villages.

So many festivals occur in this little country that one may easily take them for granted. The major event of all festivals and competitions is the yearly Concours International Reine Elisabeth, named for the music-loving Belgian queen, Elisabeth. Prizes are awarded alternately in competitions for violinists, pianists, or composers. Audiences attend all rounds from the first elimination through the finals.

Besides Brussels, several other centers of musical activity exist in Belgium. In opera houses in Antwerp, Ghent, Liège, Mons, Namur, Tournai, and Verviers, the opera season generally runs from September to May. In some cities, Antwerp for example, all-time favorites such as *Madama Butterfly* and *Lohengrin* will be offered regularly in Flemish; and, in addition, the operas of local composers, both past and present, will be staged during the season. The Belgians are shrewd businessmen, and they will seek to cater to the tastes of their local audiences. Maurice Huisman, of Brussels' Théâtre Royal de la Monnaie, has been making tremendous strides in bringing younger audiences into the opera houses. He does it by means of novelty and mixed media productions, as well as lowered prices and convenient Sunday and holiday performances. Antwerp, Blankenberghe, Charleroi, Dinant, Knokke-Het-Zoute, Namur, Oostende, and Spa all support concert halls.

Of course, the Palais des Beaux-Arts in Brussels has one of the finest concert halls in Europe, and the Théâtre Royal de la Monnaie, the opera house built on the site of the old Mint, is one of the architectural gems of Europe. It is also of major historical significance for its performances. A showing of *La Muette de Portici* on August 25, 1830, precipitated the start of the Belgian Revolution of Independence. Puppet shows similar to those in Germany and Austria are offered in Antwerp, Brussels, Ghent, and Liège. Historical pageants that include music are given in courtyards of castles, abbeys, historic mansions, and marketplaces of medieval towns.

Governed in turn by the Romans, the French, the Austrians, the Dutch, and the Spanish, with return visits by the Austrians, French, and Dutch, Belgium today is among the youngest of the independent nations of Western

Europe, earning her final independence from Holland in 1830. Despite her youth, however, the country today is the virtual economic focus of Europe, and supports the pursuit of culture to an extent that is the envy of musicians in other countries more than twice her size.

New Area Codes and Telephone Numbers in Belgian Cities

A short while ago, telephone numbers in Brussels started including seven digits instead of six. Where possible, we have indicated the new phone number. Any Brussels phone number with six digits is an older number; when given to the operator he/she will tell you which additional digit should precede it.

Phone numbers in cities outside of Brussels added one digit to the area code, although the area code for Brussels remains the same. Below you will find a list of these new area codes by cities.

Aalst 053	Ieper 057	Tournai 069
Arlon 063	Komen 056	Veurne 058
Antwerp 031	Kortrijk 056	Verviers 087
Ath 068	Liège 041	Waremme 019
Barvaux 086	La Louvière 064	Wavre 010
Brugge 050	Librament 061	
Bastogne 062	Leuven 016	
Charleroi 071	Mechelen 015	
Chimay 060	Mons 065	
Ciney 083	Marche 084	
Dendermonde 052	Nivelles 067	
Diest 013	Ninove 054	
Dinant 082	Oostende 059	
Ghent 091	Roeselare 051	
Huy 085	Ronse 055	
Hasselt 011	Stavelot 080	
Herentals 014	Tongeren 012	

Guides and Services

The Belgian National Tourist Office, Brussels   Tel: 13 90 90
7 gare Centrale, boulevard de l'Impératrice
This office provides information on all of Belgium. Among the numerous items available to you when you visit them are a *Calendar of Touristic Events* (in English), *Artistic Belgium,* and many other brochures and pamphlets that will prove helpful.

The Brussels Information Service
12 rue de la Colline, just off the Grand' Place   Tel: 11 88 88
Hours: daily from 9:00 AM to 9:00 PM in summer; from 9:00 AM to 7:00 PM in
    winter.
Other offices with shorter hours will be found in the Hôtel de Ville and at the
building at 10 rue de Chêne.

Belgian Tourist Office (USA)
720 Fifth Avenue, New York, N.Y. 10019   Tel: (212) 582-1750

Belgian Information Service (USA)
50 Rockefeller Plaza, New York, N.Y. 10017   Tel: (212) 586-5110

Principal Events in Belgium (in English)
From either of the two American offices listed above, you may order gratis this
pamphlet that appears annually. It includes a diary of events taking place in
Belgium throughout the year. Music and theater, special local events, carillon
concerts, organ concerts, art exhibitions, and sports events are covered. Trade
fairs and congresses are also detailed.

NATIONAL HOLIDAYS

January	1	New Year's Day
April	*	Easter Monday
May	1	Labor Day
	*	Ascension Day
	*	Whit Monday
July	21	National Day
November	1	All Saints' Day
	11	Armistice Day
December	25	Christmas

* = movable

BRUSSELS   Tel. prefix: (02)

Brussels is a fascinating city that all too often gets short shrift from American
visitors planning their vacations abroad. To some, Brussels is the economic
capital of Europe, seat of NATO, SATO, the EEC, etc. It is also headquarters
for more American companies based abroad than any other city of comparable

size. Chic, sophisticated, and cosmopolitan, the inhabitants of Brussels would feel at home in any other capital city of Europe or the States. In their finest restaurants the food is better and more reasonably priced than in Paris, and the service is unbelievably courteous. Their cultural efforts often exceed those of their much wealthier neighbors—mainly because of a "We'll-show-them" attitude. Smaller, more intimate, and less beautiful than Paris because she strives constantly to improve herself, Brussels usually succeeds.

In order to compete, the Bruxellois make every effort to foster musical life with concerts, and avant-garde programs on the radio and even at the opera. Their ballet (see below) has become internationally famous. As early as the beginning of the twentieth century, the Libre-Esthétique was the scene of first performances of new music by Albéniz, de Falla, Debussy, and Ravel. Today, intent on reaching the young and thus building new audiences, a recent innovation by the management of the Palais des Beaux-Arts accounted for a complete renovation of one of their auditoriums into what is now called the Salle M. An exposition hall for young artists to show their wares, the Salle is also the place for the younger generation to congregate, converse, and choose their evening or afternoon entertainment from among the many advertised there.

Curiously, although it is very much a commercial center, Brussels offers its visitors (and its citizens, too) the delightful paradox of a modern-day city literally surrounded by an enchanted forest, the Forêt de Soignies, which is not more than twenty minutes from any point in the center of the city. For ethnomusicologists, the wonderful Royal Central Africa Museum on the edge of another five hundred-acre park (Tervuren) affords a constant reminder of Belgium's role in Africa. Non-Western instruments are on display throughout the museum.

Many museums in Brussels close at 4:00 PM during the winter and stay open until 5:00 PM in the summer. Most museums are closed on Mondays. Check with the Tourist Office or the local papers before starting out.

For art *nouveau* architecture, visit the Baron Horta House at 25 Rue Américaine (2:00 PM to 5:00 PM except Tuesdays; admission is free). Other house facades worth a look are at 11 Square Ambiorix, 5 Rue de Francs, and the flower shop at 13 Rue Royale.

For the numerous performances in churchyards and cathedrals, it is also best to check local guides and newspapers for time. One annual occurrence is not to be missed: every Christmas day at St. Michael's, Belgium's national church, there is a performance of Berlioz's *L'Enfance du Christ* staged with puppets and performers on stilts. It is a spectacle that cannot be described adequately in words, but must be seen. The new library complex (see below for Albert Ier Bibliothèque) and the marionette performances at the Toone (see below) are other specialties of this city that deserve more attention than they get.

Several years ago, Drew Middleton wrote an article for *The New York Times* in which he stated that Brussels today is two cities: one is the capital of Europe, site of the European Economic Community (Common Market), and head-quarters of the North Atlantic Treaty Organization. As such it is a magnet for banks, brokers, law firms, diplomats, reporters, and entrepreneurs from both sides of the Atlantic. The other city is old Brussels.

For our part, we're interested mostly in the libraries, collections, castles, concert halls, cathedrals, and monuments of old Brussels. From another point of view, the fact that Brussels has so many American and international firms resident there makes the number of English-language guidebooks and materials more numerous here than anywhere else. Here is a trilingual list:

Guides and Services

The Bulletin: The Belgian Weekly in English
38 place Grand Sablon   Tel: 513 91 28; 513 42 83
Everything you need or want to know about Brussels and environs concerning entertainment (concerts, opera, theater, ballet, sports, marionettes) as well as shopping and services will be found within these pages. The *Bulletin* may be purchased at newsstands or at the major hotels and book stores.

The Brussels Times (an American Guide)
59 rue du Prince Royal   Tel: 12 56 44
Editor David T. Hayhaw's comments on the Brussels scene are apparently more to the liking of the natives than those found in the English *Bulletin*. This guide appears regularly on Thursdays and is also available at the major hotels and newsstands.

Bruxelles Agenda (in French and Flemish)
1000 rue du Chêne   Tel: 13 41 77
Less comprehensive than the English-language *Bulletin* and *The Brussels Times, Bruxelles Agenda* is a weekly entertainment guide on sale at newsstands, book stores, hotels, and at the Centre d'Information de Bruxelles at 12 rue de la Colline (just off the Grand' Place).

Bruxelles Scope: Agenda et Critique des Spectacles
9 rue de la Mignon   Tel: 33 36 49
Bruxelles Scope is a French-language publication that appears twice monthly. It contains an entertainment guide and a few critical articles.

A paperback, *Brussels Walk Guide*, written by Anne Fuller Dillon and Patricia Marini Samson, published by Edts. J. Malvaux, 69 rue Delaunoy, 1080 Brussels, appeared in March 1972. It is far and away the best and most comprehensive English-language guide to the city. You will find it at major newsstands and book stores. This guide cannot be recommended highly enough.

Opera Houses and Concert Halls

Théâtre Royal de la Monnaie (l'Opéra, or TRM)
4 rue Leopold   Tel: 217 22 11; 218 12 02
Season: August 1 to June 30. Opera and ballet.
Box Office Hours: daily 11:00 AM to 7:00 PM.
Seating Capacity: 1100.
There are eighty affiliated ticket agencies in Belgium.

It was an Italian financier and diplomat, Gio-Paolo Bombarda, who founded the Théâtre Royal de la Monnaie. As a representative of the Elector of Bavaria, he arrived in the Netherlands in 1693, married Gertrude Marie Cloots (member of a prominent Antwerp banking family) in Amsterdam, and proceeded soon afterward to buy property in Brussels. Always interested in the stage, he arranged for the construction of the Théâtre in 1699 on the site of the old Mint. Opened in 1700, the Théâtre initially offered the finest theatrical entertainments, both foreign and domestic.

By about 1815, the theater had fallen on hard times, and in May 1819, a new building was constructed in front of the old one, which was demolished the following year. Beginning at this time, foreign operas, particularly those by Rossini, became popular. Weber's *Freischütz* was performed here as *Robin des bois* in 1825. February 12, 1829, Auber's *La Muette de Portici* had a successful première, but the authorities tried to keep it off the boards. Remounted on August 24, 1830, its performance actually precipitated the Belgian Revolution of that year. In 1855, the edifice was destroyed by fire, but rebuilt the following year.

Today, the Théâtre Royal de la Monnaie, or l'Opéra as it is called, is one of the most successful in Europe. It has a relatively small permanent company and hires foreign singers regularly. Many Americans sing there each season. In a recent interview, Maurice Huisman, the director, mentioned that twelve young singers work fulltime with the opera, and twelve apprentice at the studio, which prepares them for possible future careers with the main house. The operas offered range from *L'incoronazione di Poppea* (Monteverdi), which we heard one Christmas eve, to *Traviata* and *Wozzeck*. *Aniara*, the Swedish opera by Blomdahl, was the first directed by the late Goeran Gentele outside his native Stockholm.

La Petite Maison, the younger company of the Théâtre, might use its singers for an avant-garde *Bohème* or for different new works. The principal aim of Director Huisman is to promote interest in opera for young people and working people—in other words, to bring in new audiences. To do this effectively, he has priced students' tickets very low and he makes seats available to workers and other groups at special prices within each price category. He does not believe in reserving a special section for workers or students. Furthermore, a première, instead of being a gala, will often be a performance for students and older persons.

Receipts account for about thirty percent of operating costs; the balance is subsidized by the government. Performances are usually excellent. The theater itself is a gem that should be seen by all who visit Brussels.

Palais des Beaux-Arts

23 rue Ravenstein   Tel: 512 50 45; 512 15 53;
                              also 511 30 66 to reserve a hall for a particular event
Season: September 1 to June.
Box Office Hours: daily except Sunday from 11:00 AM to 7:00 PM. Tel: 512 50 45
Seating Capacity: 2200 in large hall where opera, ballet, and theatrical performances are given; 620 in smaller hall for chamber music; 250 in recital hall for films and plays; 150 in small theater.
The Palais is an enormous building resembling the old Madison Square Garden in New York City. The center of the cultural life of Brussels, its architect was Baron V. Horta, the so-called specialist in "modern" architecture. The Palais publishes a monthly performance guide—actually two, one in French and one in Flemish—listing the days and hours of each presentation as well as the locations. In addition to the four different halls listed above, there are three other rooms where entertainments of various kinds are presented. Besides musical and dramatic events, lectures, poetry readings, etc., are presented here.
There are five different sections of the Palais des Beaux-Arts. For correspondence, it is sufficient to write to the address listed above, but you must list which theater you are interested in—the simple designation, "Music," "Ballet," etc., will suffice.

Société Philharmonique de Bruxelles

Palais des Beaux-Arts, 11 rue Baron Horta   Tel: 512 10 01; 512 10 02
Season: September to June; no annual closing dates. Closed on legal holidays.
Box Office: Palais des Beaux-Arts, 23 rue Ravenstein.
Hours: 11:00 AM to 7:00 PM daily except Sunday.
Authorized Ticket Agencies: Banque Lambert, Banque de Bruxelles, Kredietbank.

Salle du Conservatoire Royal de Musique de Bruxelles

30a rue de la Régence   Tel: 512 23 69; 511 04 27
Season: October 1 to Easter, presenting concerts, recitals, musicals and plays.
Box Office: open Monday to Friday, 9:00 AM to noon, 2:00 PM to 5:00 PM.
Seating Capacity: 800.

Concerts du Midi ASBL

27 rue Ducale   Tel: 511 93 13
Season: October to May, presenting chamber music.
Seating Capacity: 650.

Concerts are given every Wednesday from 12:40 PM to 1:00 PM in the Salle Rubens of the Musée d'Art Ancien, 3 rue de la Régence.

Cirque Royal (Koninklijk Circus)
81 rue de l'Enseignement   Tel: 26 98 63
Season: September to May with the annual closing variable; ballets and "Variétés" are presented.
Box Office Hours: days on which there are performances from 10:00 AM to 7:00 PM.   Tel: 218 20 15; 218 22 60
Seating Capacity: 2200.

Maison de la Musique
39 rue Lebeau   Tel: 512 04 49
Season: September 15 to July 15, presenting concerts every Tuesday for adults and young persons' concerts for children aged 6 to 10.
Seating Capacity: 80-100.

Centre Culturel et Artistique d'Uccle
47 rue Rouge   Tel: 374 04 95; 374 04 96
Season: open all year presenting opera, ballet, and concerts with facilities for conventions and banquets.
Box Office: open 11:00 AM to 5:00 PM daily except Sunday.   Tel: 374 64 84
Seating Capacity: Salle spectacles 803; concert 500; banquet 450.

Other ticket agencies are:
1. Centre d'information de Bruxelles, 12 rue de la Colline. Daily 11:00 AM to 5:00 PM. Closed Sunday.
2. Secretariat artistique de la Société Générale de Banque "Armentor," 61 avenue Louise. Daily except Saturday and Sunday, 9:00 AM to noon and 2:00 PM to 5:00 PM.
3. L'Otan Bureau de Madame Questiaux. For members only from 12:30 PM to 2:30 PM. This organization also publishes a monthly called *Le Wolvendael*, obtainable from above address. Its approximately fifty pages carry entertainment news of the area as well as many advertisements. Available on subscription. (See above for more periodicals and concert guides.)

Marionette Theaters

Toone
21-23 Petite rue des Bouchers, 6 Impasse Schuddeveld   Tel: 511 71 37
One of Brussels' most famous marionette theaters, this company has been in the same family for generations. Large puppets appear in performances that range from *Faust* and the Passion Play to *Le Cid* and the numerous plays written

specifically for the troupe by de Ghelderode (see his workroom, a replica of which appears in the National Museum and Library). The Brussels dialect in use here may be difficult for foreigners, but the gestures and situations themselves make almost everything understandable. Performances are given every evening except Sunday, at 8:30 PM.

Théâtre des Coeurs de Bois
16 rue Dekens   Tel: 733 87 01
Performances on Wednesday, Saturday, Sunday at 3:00 PM. For summer performances in Parc de Roodebeek, check newspapers or telephone.

Théâtre de l'Enfance (part of Toone)
21-23 Petite rue des Bouchers   Tel: 211 71 73; 217 27 53
Performances on Wednesday and Sunday at 3:00 and 4:00 PM for children aged 2 to 8.

Théâtre du Perruchet
50 avenue de la Forêt   Tel: 673 87 30
Performances on Wednesday, Saturday, Sunday at 3:00 PM from September to end of May.

Libraries and Museums

"There are no independent music libraries in Belgium. A music library is either part of a larger library, or it is connected to a musical institute. More or less complete and accurate inventories exist only in the larger libraries, such as the Royal Library, the university libraries, the libraries of the Royal Conservatories and the main Public Libaries." So wrote Kamiel Cooremans of Ghent in an article on Belgium's Music Libraries in *Fontes Artis Musicae* (1975), the journal of the International Association of Music Libraries. Since then the same journal has put out an entire issue (Vol. XXIII, 1976/3) on music publishers, libraries, and instrument collections in Belgium.

Archives de la Ville, Hôtel de Ville [Ben. 12]
Grand' Place   Tel: 513 48 62
Hours: Monday to Friday, 9:00 AM to 11:45 PM, 1:30 PM to 5:15 PM. Closed
    August 15-31. Users must be 18 years of age or older.
Facilities: no reproduction equipment available; some working space.
Contains about 3000 items, one of the most important theatrical collections in Europe, with approximately 477 opera scores, 115 ballet scores, most of the holdings related to Brussels theaters, particularly a collection of eighteenth- and nineteenth-century opera scores and libretti that belong to the Théâtre de la

Monnaie (see above); works of contemporary Belgians as well as earlier masters; a collection of plays (about 404 historical items) as well. The Archives also sponsors a series of publications.

Koninklijke Bibliotheek Albert I (Bibliothèque Royale Albert Ier)[Ben. 13]
4 boulevard de l'Empereur   Tel: 513 61 80
Hours: Monday to Saturday, 9:00 AM to noon and 2:00 PM to 5:00 PM. Closed the week before Easter.
This library is the country's only copyright depository for books and written records.

(CeBeDeM) (Centre Belge de Documentation Musicale) [Ben. 14]
31 rue de l' Hôpital   Tel: 512 49 87
Hours: Monday to Friday, 9:00 AM to 5:00 PM. Closed January 1, Easter Monday, May 1, Ascension Day, Whit Monday, July 21 to August 21, November 1 and November 11, December 25.
This extraordinary institution is an independent center supported by the Ministry of Culture. The CeBeDeM tries to promote Belgian contemporary music at home and abroad. It is responsible for catalogs of over two dozen Belgian composers; it reproduces unpublished music, and it provides information on written request.

Its library and listening room are open to the public, and no charge is made for the reference service. Music may be obtained on approval; it is also sold or loaned. All catalogs are free on request. The CeBeDeM is similar in function to the Donemus organization in The Netherlands (see below).

Essentially the library is the repository of performing scores and parts of works (published and unpublished) by contemporary Belgians. It also has a collection of press clippings, biographical information, and a tape and record library. A nonprofit organization, the CeBeDeM, founded by private initiative, was soon placed under the auspices of the Belgian Ministry of Culture. The Center compiles lists of the works of its members, reproduces unpublished scores for performance, provides orchestral material for performances, and information on affiliated composers. The Center is of course associated with the International Association of Music Libraries.

Bibliothèque du Conservatoire Royal de Musique [Ben. 15]
30 rue de la Régence   Tel: 511 04 27; 12 23 69
Hours: Monday to Friday 9:00 AM to noon, 2:00 PM to 5:00 PM during class sessions. Closed for school vacations on Christmas, Easter, July 15 to October 1.

Musée Instrumental du Conservatoire Royal de Bruxelles
17 place du Petit Sablon   Tel: 513 25 54
(Entrance around the corner from the Conservatoire)

Hours: Tuesday, Thursday, Saturday 2:30 PM to 4:30 PM; Sunday 10:30 AM to 12:30 PM; Wednesday 8:00 PM to 10:00 PM with recitals given on instruments of the Museum. Closed January 1, April 12, May 1, May 20, May 31, July 21, August 15, November 1, November 11, December 25. Admission is free, but a recommendation is necessary for research on instruments. Admission is also free to the concerts given here.

This museum occupies several floors of a beautiful old building adjoining the Conservatoire and overlooking one of the most delightful squares in Brussels. The instruments are well displayed and carefully labeled. Professor Roger Bragard, the former curator of the museum, and Dr. Ferdinand J. De Hen, a specialist in organology, the history of musical instruments, have together produced an excellent volume, *Musical Instruments in Art and History* (English edition, New York: Viking Press, 1968), that includes color plates of many of the prized possessions of the museum. Also available are two records: one of early music and one of folk music, both prepared on instruments of the collection.

The collection itself originated in 1872 when the Conservatoire acquired seventy-four instruments from the estate of the recently deceased director of the Conservatoire, the musicologist J.F. Fétis. Four years later, ninety-eight Indian instruments were offered the Belgian king, Leopold II, by the Raja Sourindro Tagore. The Instrument Museum was established in 1877 with the renowned organologist Victor-Charles Mahillon as its first curator. This constantly expanding collection is one of the richest in the world.

Bibliothèque de la Radiodiffusion-Television Belge (RTB)
18 place Eugène Flagey   Tel: 49 22 80; 49 60 50
One of the best working music libraries will be found here at the radio station. Mme. Adrienne Doignies-Musters is in charge of this organization. Together with her able assistant Jean Ferrard, music librarian and organist par excellence, she has accumulated a collection of complete works *(Gesamtausgaben)* as well as considerable contemporary music that is available on loan to other radio stations and performing organizations. To date, the collection includes about 20,000 symphony parts, 3200 vocal scores, 10,000 vocal parts, 4000 orchestral scores, 135 opera scores. The library houses the Centre de Documentation of the EBU (European Broadcasting Union). It has a central catalog of all symphonic materials in the libraries of thirty-one broadcasting systems.

Bibliothèque de la Société Philharmonique
80 rue Artan
Write to M. Hervé Thys, the Director of the Philharmonic Society of Brussels, for information and access.

Bibliothèque de l'Université Libre de Bruxelles
Faculté de Philosophie et Lettres-Séminaire de Musicologie
50 avenue Franklin Roosevelt

Discothèque Nationale de Belgique (to borrow records)
Administration Centrale: 320 Chaussée de Vleurgat
44 Passage
Home base for this discotheque is Brussels, but there are branches throughout the country. The facilities are rapidly expanding in order to meet the demands of those who use them. All together are responsible for the numerous record buses which tour the countryside making current LP records available to people living in rural areas who cannot get to the libraries.

A borrower from any branch of the Discothèque Nationale de Belgique pays about $5.00 for the first two years that he is a member. After that time, he becomes a life member. Records are loaned at a charge of one-thirtieth of their retail price. (We must remember, however, that record prices in European countries are substantially higher than in the States!)

The Discothèque also presents educational television shows and radio broadcasts. Their collection includes classical records, a good selection of folk music, carefully selected jazz, spoken word recordings, children's records, but no pop music. Recordmobiles (buses) visit each town in Belgium about twice monthly.

Deutsche Bibliothek Brussel (A branch of the Goethe Institute)
58 rue Belliard   Tel: 512 78 70
Record Library Hours: Wednesday, 11:00 AM to 7:00 PM; Tuesday, Thursday, Friday, 11:00 AM to 1:00 PM. Main Library: Tuesday to Friday, 11:00 AM to 7:00 PM; Saturday, 11:00 AM to 1:00 PM. Closed July and August, and December 20 to January 6.

Conservatories and Schools

Conservatoire Royal de Musique de Bruxelles
30 rue de la Régence   Tel: 512 23 69; 511 04 27
The Koninklijk Muziekconservatorium at 30 Regentiestraat, the Flemish equivalent of the organization described above, has its own staff and administration, and director Kamiel d'Hooghe is in charge here. (Notice that even the address looks different in Flemish!)

The Conservatoire Royal de Musique, under the auspices of the Ministry of Culture, publishes an informative brochure that will be sent on request. You will learn, for example, that applicants for admission must be no more than 18 years of age if they intend to study piano or stringed instruments; 20 for organ and winds; 22 for girls and 26 for boys for voice and dramatic arts.

As in France, nationality is important. Foreigners are admitted, but must receive written authorization from the Ministry of Culture. Netherlanders and citizens of Luxembourg are considered natives. Although students have the right to request specific professors as their teachers, the Director reserves the right of final decision in such matters. Tuition is free.

Musical Landmarks

The composer **Joseph Jongen** (1873–1953) is buried in the cemetery at Uccle (Brussels); a monument to him is at the Conservatoire Royal, and his cottage is at Sart-lez-Spa in the Ardennes.

Although recently demolished, the *Café des Boulevards,* place Charles Rogier, Brussels, was the center for the Cercle des Arts, a group of artists led by **Bériot** (see below) and including **François Servais, Liszt, Thalberg,** and **Henri Herz,** as well as the painters **J.B. Madou** and **A. Quetelet.**

The home of **Charles de Bériot** (1802–1870), composer and violinist, and husband of the famous singer **Maria Malibran,** is located at 13 avenue de l'Astronomie, 1030 Brussels. Hours: daily from 8:00 AM to 5:00 PM. Closed Sundays and holidays.

Note that the paintings, sculptures, and personal memorabilia belonging to de Bériot are not here; they are on display at the Musée Charlier, 16 avenue des Arts. This museum has a different schedule of opening times: daily 9:30 AM to 12:30 PM except Sunday. A guide is available on request. Contact Mme. Ketels, archivist of the museum, at Tel: 218 53 82.

Among the poets and writers associated with musicians, a few lived in Brussels at one time or another in their lives. **Charles Baudelaire** (1821–1867) whose texts were set often by French musicians including **Debussy, Fauré** and **Duparc,** lived in Brussels from 1864 at the Hôtel du Grand Miroir, near the celebrated Grand' Place.

George Gordon, Lord Byron (1788–1824), whose works inspired **Schumann** and **Berlioz,** lived in Brussels for a while in 1816 at the fashionable hotel No. 51 rue Ducale. In 1924, a plaque was put at the entrance of this building.

Paul Verlaine (1844–1896), the symbolist poet whose text provided the basis for **Fauré's** cycle, *La Bonne Chanson,* was taken to the Amigo Prison here, after shooting his friend and fellow poet, **Arthur Rimbaud.**

A replica of the workroom of the famous Flemish poet **Émile Verhaerem** (1855–1916) is located in the room for special collections of the Belgian National Library. Verhaeren's *Hélène de Sparthe* was the basis of **Séverac's** *La Fille de la terre.*

Musical Organizations

Fédération Internationale des Jeunesses Musicales
5 rue Baron Horta   Tel: 511 49 21
The Belgian branch of Jeunesses Musicales is located at 10 rue Royale.
Tel: 513 97 74
Jeunesses Musicales is an international movement which encourages youth and young adults to participate in the musical life of their country as performers, composers, and critics.

The major goal of Jeunesses Musicales is to bring artists, ensembles, and speakers to local chapters of its respective countries. It also encourages the careers of gifted young artists through awards, etc. In many countries, Jeunesses Musicales publishes a national magazine for its members and holds an annual congress to discuss plans for the new year. In some countries, the organization also runs music camps, publishes new compositions, issues recordings, and broadcasts special programs.

Marcel Cuvelier initiated the movement in Belgium in 1940; almost simultaneously, René Nicoly, who is today honorary president of the international movement, began a Jeunesses Musicales in France. After this, the Jeunesses Musicales spread rapidly through Europe and, later, to other continents.

In each country, Jeunesses Musicales is a self-governing organization; it must, however, abide by certain standards fixed by the Fédération Internationale des Jeunesses Musicales, in which all national groups are equally represented, with headquarters in Brussels.

Ministère de l'Éducation National et de la Culture, Direction des Arts Musicaux et Lyriques (see Flemish equivalent below)
158 avenue de Cortenberg   Tel: 735 21 77

Ministerie Van Nationale Opvoeding en Kultuur, Directie voor Muziek en Lyrische Kunst
158 Kortenberglaan   Tel: 735 61 40

Académie Royale de Sciences, Lettres, et Beaux-Arts de Belgique
Palais des Académies, 1 rue Ducale   Tel: 512 73 23

Koninklijke Vlaamse Academie voor Wetenschappen, Letteren, en Schone Kunsten
Paleis der Academiën, 1 Hertogstraat

SACEM (Société des Auteurs, Compositeurs, et Éditeurs Musique
54 rue du Méridien   Tel: 511 18 10

Chambre Syndicale des Éditeurs de Musique
66 rue Montagne-aux-Herbes-Potagères

Conseil National de la Musique
Palais des Beaux-Arts, 11 rue Baron Horta

Société Belge de Musicologie
30 rue de la Régence

Centre de Sociologie de la Musique
44 avenue Jeanne

La Confédération Musicale de Belgique
10 P. Havwaerts Square   Tel: 241 36 65

Union des Chefs d'Orchestre de Belgique
48 rue Malibran

Symphony Orchestras

Grand Orchestre Symphonique de l'Institut National de Radiodiffusion
18 place Eugène Flagey

Orchestre de Chambre des Concerts du Midi
27 rue Ducale

Orchestre de Chambre du Théâtre Royal de la Monnaie
Place de la Monnaie

Orchestre National de Belgique
Ministère de l'Instruction Publique
155 rue de la Loi   Tel: 733 94 55; 734 13 91

Miscellaneous

Educational Institutions that Guide Travelers

Brussels

Belgian-Luxembourg School Journeys, 169 rue de la Loi.
Ministry of Public Instruction, Educational Services, Residence Palace, 155 rue de la Loi.
National Youth Service, 158 avenue de Cortenberg.
Students' Friends, 21 rue de Medaets.
Voyages Scolaires Belgo-Luxembourgeois.

The Business of Music

Secondhand Book Stores

La Porte Étroite, R. Daubies
   13 rue Duquesnoy

Librairie Moens, A. Leclercq
   27–29 rue Saint Jean
   Always ask for *"des ouvrages sur la musique."* You might also try the Flea Market in the place du Jeu de Balle, open daily from 8:00 AM to 1:00 PM.

Les Amis de la Musique
   17 avenue des Staphylins   Tel: 672 03 23

Flea Market
   Place du Jeu de Balle
   Held every day of the week from 8:00 AM to 1:00 PM. There are no covered stalls here and merchandise is spread out on the square. Little treasures can be found that are usually of no great value, but of no great cost either!

Antique and Book Market
   22 rue Bodenbroeck
   Twenty different dealers have stalls under one roof, at Au Rouet, 22 rue Bodenbroeck. The market is held from 9:00 AM to 6:00 PM on Saturdays, and from 9:00 AM to 1:00 PM on Sundays and holidays.

   A Sunday morning "special" finds two different antique markets a bare ten-minute walk apart. At Place du Jeu de Balle (see above) in the Marolles quarter of Brussels, you'll find Brussels' brand of kitsch. At place du Grand Sablon, the dealers whose shops surround the square move their wares into tents in the courtyard of the church of Notre-Dame-du-Sablon. Open all day Saturday as well as Sunday mornings. Dealers here don't take kindly to haggling. Pay what they ask. They have the best merchandise.

Publishers

Brogneaux (Mme J-B Faulx)
   73 avenue Paul Janson
Cranz
   22 rue d'Assaut
Hulpiau
   122 rue de la Clinique
Henry Lemoine
   37 boulevard du Jardin Botanique
J. Maurer
   7 avenue du Verseau   Tel: 770 93 39
Melodia (Mr. Edgard Maes)
   13 Jean Heymansstraat
Polfliet
   13 rue Wayez   Tel: 512 83 71
Schott Frères
   30 rue Saint Jean   Tel: 512 39 80
Vriamont
   25 rue de la Régence
Éditions Culture et Civilisations (reprints)
   115 avenue Gabriel Lebon

Instrument Makers: Pianos

Van der Elst
   184 rue Royale   Tel: 217 33 50; 217 99 00
Gunther
   184 rue Royale   Tel: 217 33 50
Pierard
   35 rue du Fort
Fauchille
   85 rue Potagère   Tel: 217 99 31
Hanlet
   5 rue de Livourne   Tel: 537 88 24
Hautrive
   271 rue Royale   Tel: 217 96 92

Huyghe
  6 rue Verwée
Knud Kaufmann (clavecins)
  81 rue Botanique   Tel: 218 38 86
Michel van Hecke (harpsichords)
  19 rue Jordaens
Jean Tournay (harpsichords)
  5 allée du Cloître
Patrick Collon (organs)
  53 rue Cloessens   Tel: 428 96 79

Instrument Makers: Stringed instruments

Lutherie d'Art
  229 chaussée de Charleroi
Luthier Anzellotti
  37 rue de Molenbeek   Tel: 425 28 87
Luthier Van der Raay
  49 rue St. Bernard   Tel: 537 86 06

Instrument Makers: Brass instruments and others

Polfliet (brass)
  57 rue du Midi   Tel: 512 83 71
Manufacture Mahillon et Cie.
  114 rue Berthelet
Persy (brass)
  76–78 rue Marché-au-Charbon   Tel: 512 35 62

Concert Managers

Association des Concerts du Conservatoire Royal de Bruxelles
  30 rue de la Régence   Tel: 511 44 95
l'Atelier
  51 rue du Commerce   Tel: 511 20 65
Paul Babick
  4 rue Saint-Christophe   Tel: 511 43 40
Centre d'Organisation de Spectacles
  19 rue du Gazomètre
G. Genske
  43 rue de Bouchers   Tel: 511 12 65
Hirsch
  10 rue Léon-Lepage   Tel: 511 11 23
Louis Kersch
  293 rue Gatti-de-Gamond   Tel: 376 65 85

Jacques Mauroy
    23 rue Ravenstein
International Artists Promotion
    129 avenue du Pesage
Pimentel Theatrical Productions
    69 avenue Louis Lepoutre   Tel: 345 31 39
Société Philharmonique de Bruxelles et Société des Concerts Populaires
Palais des Beaux-Arts
    11 rue Baron Horta   Tel: 512 10 01
Monsieur Jacques Vaerewyck, Directeur de l'Association pour la Diffusion
Artistique et Culturelle, Activités Internationales
Palais des Beaux-Arts
    10 rue Royale   Tel: 513 87 50

Music Dealers

Schott Frères
    30 rue Saint Jean   Tel: 512 39 80
    Music, records, instruments.
Corman Librairie
    28–30 rue Ravenstein   Tel: 511 67 29
    General bookstore that carries music books.
Office International de Librairies
    30 avenue Marnix & 5 rue Luxembourg   Tel: 513 66 75
    General bookstore that carries music books.

ANTWERP (Anvers)   Tel. prefix: (031)

Despite its significance both as an international seaport and as the diamond
center of Europe, Antwerp gives the visitor the impression of being a small
town. Like many of the Flemish cities of Belgium, it combines elements of the
past with much of the present. Fiercely proud of their city, the citizens recognize
it as the de facto Flemish capital, rival in its own way to Brussels. Flemish is the
principal language spoken, but many people speak English. (Don't try French
first when you approach a native. He will probably recognize your accent and
reply immediately in English.)

Whatever these people do, they act with great determination and much
enthusiasm. We recall with pleasure a Sunday afternoon performance of
Madama Butterfly, presented in Flemish and directed by a German *Intendant* from
Munich. A Yugoslav maestro conducted the orchestra, and a Czech régisseur

recently arrived from his homeland arranged the staging (using French to communicate with his colleagues). All these nationals worked together under the kind but firm direction of Rennat Verbruggen, Flemish director of the Antwerp Schouwburg. Opera in this city is always in the vernacular.

In Ghent, however, the other large Flemish city, operas are presented in their original language. The chorus as well as the orchestra personnel and several of the soloists are all trained locally in Antwerp's schools and conservatories. Diversified productions include the classics from Mozart to Verdi as well as contemporary Dutch operas and ballets. It is relatively difficult for Americans to learn their roles in Flemish and for this reason we did not find many of our own singers on the roster. Germans and Scandinavians have fewer problems with the language, and consequently, visiting singers from these countries appear here often.

Antwerp has ten theaters and two music halls, besides the opera house. Goldmuntz Hall, a very modern auditorium in the Jewish Community Center, is now used for recitals of avant-garde music and theater. Antwerp has a large Jewish community, many of whom are in the diamond trade. Although numbers of Jews fled Belgium before the arrival of the Germans, some of them returned to their homeland after 1945. Many who went underground were saved through the efforts of their Belgian countrymen. In showing their gratitude, they have provided considerable support for cultural activities here.

While Ghent and Bruges are the two other well-known Flemish cities whose artistic treasures make them internationally famous, it is to Antwerp that the Flemings turn for leadership, regarding the city as the metropolis of their country.

Guides and Services

Dienst voor Toerisme (City Tourist Office)
19 Suikerrui
Any letters of inquiry (in English) are promptly answered. For visitors, this office is located in front of the rail station.

Antwerpen

Obtainable at the office listed above, contains information on all activities, including cultural ones.

Maandkalender van der Stad Antwerpen (Monthly calendar in Dutch, but the significant information can readily be understood.)

Sponsored by the city and published by its tourist office, this calendar can be purchased at the office or at your hotel. The publication includes articles on local festivities, concerts, visiting artists, etc. You may request it in advance, by mail.

Opera Houses and Concert Halls

Arenbergschouwburg
28 Arenbergstraat   Tel: 32 11 14; 32 85 23
Season: September to June, presenting theater, concerts, ballets, recitals.
Box Office: open 11:00 AM to 5:00 PM daily except Sunday.   Tel: 32 85 23
Seating Capacity: 815.
There are no authorized ticket agencies other than the theater box office.

Koninklijke Vlaamse Opera (Royal Flemish Opera)
8 Van Ertbornstraat   Tel: 33 13 23
Season: mid-September to mid-June, presenting opera and ballet.
Box Office: open 11:00 AM to 3:00 PM daily, except Monday.   Tel: 33 66 85
Seating Capacity: 1000.
This theater is in the style of some of the very old Broadway houses, but the facilities backstage are quite remarkable. Almost all operas are given in Flemish.

In 1963, on the occasion of the seventieth anniversary of the opening of the house, Director Verbruggen prepared a booklet with articles about the opera, its singers and directors through the years, and its presentations since 1893.

This company travels regularly, both within the country and abroad. It has twenty-five soloists and usually about thirty-five guest artists performing with them each season. The permanent orchestra consists of about sixty-five musicians and the chorus numbers sixty. The opera receives two-thirds of its support from the city and one-third from the government. It expects in the future to have the support divided equally between the city and the nation. A performance that is a highlight in the annals of the house is the 1914 performance of *Parsifal,* one of the first (according to director Verbruggen) outside of Bayreuth.

Until fifteen years ago, the opera orchestra also performed in concerts. Now, however, the Antwerp Philharmonic has taken over that responsibility.

Rubenshuis (Rubens' House)
9-11 Rubensstraat   Tel: 32 47 51; 32 47 47
Season: July, and September to March, presenting concerts of early music on
        Sunday afternoons at 4:00 PM.
Seating Capacity: 240.
Rubens built this house for himself in 1613-1617 and lived here until his death

in 1640. The only remains of the original building are the pretty doorway in the courtyard and the summer house.

Libraries and Museums

See also the note at the beginning of Belgium General, Libraries and Museums, for further sources of information.

Archief en Museum voor het Vlaamse Cultuurleven (Archive and Museum of Flemish Cultural Life) [Ben. 1]
22 Minderbroedersstraat   Tel: 32 55 80
Hours: Monday to Friday, 8:30 AM to 4:30 PM. Closed January 1, February 1, May 1, November 1 and 2, December 25 and 26.

Koninklijk Vlaams Muziekconservatorium (Royal Flemish Conservatory of Music), Bibliotheek [Ben. 4]
25 Desquinlei   Tel: 38 31 93
Hours: Monday to Friday, 9:30 AM to noon, 2:00 PM to 5:30 PM, and Saturday morning. Closed July 15 to September 20.

Collection Persoons (Private Library of Guido Persoons) [Ben. 7]
76 Belpairestraat   Tel: 30 40 99

Stadsarchief (City Archives) [Ben. 8]
11 Venusstraat   Tel: 31 54 11;31 54 12
Hours: Monday to Friday, 8:30 AM to 4:30 PM.

Stedelijke Bibliotheken (Municipal Library) [Ben. 9]
4 Hendrik Conscienceplein   Tel: 32 30 73; 33 55 15

Verwilt, F. (Private Library) [Ben. 10]
252 Groenendaallaan   Tel: 41 19 96

Museum Vleeshuis
38-40 Vleeshouwersstraat   Tel: 33 64 04
Hours: 10:00 AM to 5:00 PM daily except Monday from September through May. Closed also January 1 and 2, May 1, Ascension Day, November 1 and 2, Christmas and Boxing Day. (Open on specific Mondays: Easter Monday: Whit Monday, and Monday after second Sunday in August.)
Seating capacity: 250.

The building also houses an important collection of musical instruments, particularly some fine harpsichords.

Conservatories and Schools

Koninklijke Vlaams Muziekconservatorium (see also *Libraries*).
25 Desquinlei (new building) and 11 St. Jacobsmarkt (old building)

Musical Landmarks

A monument to the most famous Flemish composer and conductor **Peter Benoit** (1834–1901) was executed by the architect Henry van de Velde at the "Harmonie" in Antwerp.

In the Schoonselhof, the municipal cemetery of Antwerp, is the grave of the late Flemish composer **Lodewijk Mortelmans** (1868–1952).

Musical Organizations

Belgische Mozartvereniging (Belgian Mozart Society)
Jef Alpaerts, 161 Belgiëlei

Concertvereniging van het Koninklijk Conservatorium van Antwerpen (Concert Society of the Royal Conservatory of Antwerp)
11 St. Jacobsmarkt

Muziekvereniging van de Koninklijke Maatschappij voor Dierkunde (Musical Association of the Royal Zoological Society)
20 Koningin Astridplein

Centrum voor Muziekopvoeding Halewijnsstichting v.z.w. (Center for Music Education of the Halewijn Foundation)
33 Van Putlei   Tel: 37 92 61

Symphony Orchestras

Orchestre des Kursaals d'Ostende et de Knokke
34 Constitutiestraat

Orchestre du Conservatoire Royal de Musique d'Anvers
Koninklijk Vlaams Conservatorium

Philharmonie van Antwerpen
20 Koningin Astridplein

Philharmonische Vereniging
38-40 Huidevettersstraat (Galerij 37a)   Tel: 32 04 17

The Business of Music

Publishers

Metropolis
    15 Van Ertbornstraat   Tel: 33 11 42
Scherzando
    20-22 Lovelingstraat   Tel: 36 57 09
De Ring
    17 Laurierstraat
Faes, G.
    74 Lombardenvestraat   Tel: 32 67 21
De Crans
    5 Blauwmoezelstraat   Tel: 32 04 64

Instrument Makers

De Prins Gebroeders
    60 Lammekenstraat   Tel: 35 77 05

Concert Managers

Association des Concerts Classiques
    105 Koninklijkelaan
Office International de Concerts et Spectacles
    38-40 Huidevettersstraat (37A)
Rencontres Musicales d'Anvers
    11 rue Saint-Vincent
Société des Concerts d'Anvers
    34 Constitutiestraat

BELGIUM, GENERAL

Opera Houses and Concert Halls

Besides Bruges, Ghent, and Liège (see below), the following cities have theaters and concert halls in which performances are given: Ath, Athus, Beringen, Bertrix, Beveren-Waas, Charleroi, Chimay, Dinant, Eeklo, Eupen, Frameries, Hasselt, Ieper, Knokke, Kortrijk (Courtrai), La Louvière, Leuwen (Louvain), Mechelen, Mons, Namur, Oostende, Roeselare,. Rumbeke, Saint Hubert, Sint-Niklaas, Spa, Tienen, Tournai, Turnhout, Verviers, Wevelgem, and Willebroek.

Bruges (Brugge)

Koninklijke Stadsschouwburg
Stadhuis Brugge   Tel: (050) 33 81 67
Season: October 1 to April 15 presenting opera, ballet, theater, concerts.
Box Office: Bespreekbureau Stadsschouwburg   Tel: 03 81 67
Hours: daily except Sunday and holidays 11:00 AM to .2:30 PM and 4:00 PM to 7:00 PM.
In this delightful city, from October to mid-June, 11:45 AM to 12:30 PM on Sundays, Wednesdays, and Saturdays there are carillon concerts. From mid-June through September, the time and the days change to 9:00 AM to 10:00 AM Mondays, Wednesdays, and Saturdays.
   Dienst voor Toerisme is located on Grote Markt.

Ghent

Koninklijke Vlaamse Opera (founded in 1840)
3 Schouwburgstraat   Tel: (09) 25 33 77
Season: mid-September to end of April.
Box Office: open daily 10:00 AM to 12:30 PM and 2:30 PM to 4:30 PM.
                                                                     Tel: 25 24 25
Seating Capacity: 1130.
Dienst voor Toerisme is located at 9 Borluutsstraat.

Liège

Théâtre Royal de Liège
Place de la Comèdie Française   Tel: (041) 23 21 71
Season: beginning of September to end of May.
Box Office Hours: daily 10:00 AM to 6:00 PM.

This theater, architecturally very much like the Odéon in Paris, is the home of the Opéra de Wallonie.

Libraries and Museums

For the most up-to-date information on Belgium's music publishers, libraries, and instrument collections, see *Fontes Artis Musicae,* vol. XXIII, 1976/3. This entire issue of the journal (published by the International Association of Music Libraries) is devoted to Belgium.

Bruges (Brugge)

Musée Gruuthuse
12 Dyver   Tel: (050) 03 61 33; 33 99 11
Hours: March 1 to September 30, daily 9:30 AM to noon, 2:00 PM to 6:00 PM.
    October 1 to February 28, daily except Tuesday, 10:00 AM to noon, 2:00 PM
    to 5:00 PM. Closed January 1.
Room 11 is a *Cabinet de Musique* including such old instruments as serpents, ophicleides, guitars, and drums; also flutes, oboes, bassoons, trumpets, horns, as well as a few Ruckers harpsichords.

Stedelijk Muziekconservatorium, Bibliotheek [Ben. 11]
23 St. Jacobstraat   Tel: (050) 33 43 91
Hours: Monday, Wednesday, 5:30 PM to 7:00 PM; Saturday, 11:00 AM to 1:00 PM,
    7:00 PM to 8:00 PM. Library mostly for conservatory students. Closed school
    vacations.

Ghent

Koninklijke Muziekconservatorium, Bibliotheek [Ben. 17]
50 Hoogport   Tel: (091) 25 15 15
Hours: Monday to Friday. Closed July 15 to August 11.

Rijksuniversiteit, Centrale Bibliotheek [Ben. 18]
9 Rozier   Tel: (091) 25 76 11
Hours: first Tuesday of October to May 14, 9:00 AM to 9:00 PM; May 15 to July
    14, 9:00 AM to 7:00 PM; July 15 to September 15, 8:30 AM to 1:30 PM;
    September 16 to first Tuesday in October, 8:30 AM to noon and 2:00 PM to
    5:00 PM. Admission only to university students and other readers 18 or over.

Stadsarchief [Ben. 20]
13 Abrahamstraat   Tel: (091) 25 32 53
Old carillon music.

Seminarie voor Muziekgeschiedenis Rijksuniversiteit Ghent
2 Blandijnberg

Liège

Jacques Bernard (Museum)
14 rue Soeurs-de-Hasque　　　　　　　　　　　Tel: (041) 23 67 00
Hours: Tuesday to Friday by appointment. Closed Saturday to Monday,
　Belgian holidays, and month of July.
This instrument collection includes about 350 pieces; a survey of the French
guitar from the sixteenth century; reconstructions of *vielles* from the fourteenth
century, as well as other (particularly bowed) instruments.

Musée Grétry
34 rue des Recollets　　　　　　　　　　　　Tel: 43 16 10
Hours: daily 11:00 AM to 12:30 PM, 2:00 PM to 5:00 PM, except Tuesday; Sunday
　and holidays, from 10:00 AM to 2:00 PM. Also open Wednesday, 7:00 PM to
　10:00 PM. Closed January 1, May 1, November 1, December 25.

Studio Ysaÿe (see *Landmarks*)
Conservatoire Royale, 14 rue Forgeur
Hours: Tuesday and Thursday, 3:00 PM to 5:00 PM.

Musée des Beaux-Arts de la Ville de Liège
34 rue de l'Académie　　　　　　　　　　　Tel: 32 07 99
Hours: 11:00 AM to 12:30 PM and 2:00 PM to 5:00 PM daily, except Tuesdays.
Ask for the *Section instrumental à cordes* (stringed instruments).

Bibliothèque des Chiroux
Maison de la Culture, place des Carmes　　　　　Tel: (041) 23 19 60
Hours: daily 8:30 AM to noon; 2:00 PM to 7:00 PM; Saturday, 8:30 AM to noon.
　Closed January 1, May 1, May 8, Ascension Day, Whit Monday, July 21,
　August 15, last Monday in September, November 1 and 2, November 11
　and 15, December 25 and 26.

Discothèque Nationale de Belgique, Section de Liège
35 rue de l'Université　　　　　　　　　　　Tel: (041) 42 53 90
This is not an information library, but a branch of the national phonograph
library (Discothèque Nationale), which has headquarters in Brussels. To
borrow records, phone 23 36 67.

Conservatoire Royal de Musique, Bibliothèque [Ben. 22]

14 rue Forgeur   Tel: (04) 23 52 23

Hours: Monday to Friday, 11:00 AM to noon; Monday, Tuesday, Thursday, Friday, 1:30 PM to 3:00 PM. Closed August and September.

Université de Liège, Bibliothèque [Ben. 23]

1 place Cockerill   Tel: (041) 42 00 80, ext. 206

Open when University has classes.

Mechelen (Malines)

Archief en Stadsbibliotheek [Ben. 25]

1 Steenweg   Tel: (01) 51 25 23

Stedelijke Openbare Bibliotheek (Municipal Public Library) [Ben. 26]

14 Gebroeders Verhaegenstraat

Hours: Monday to Sunday, 9:00 AM to noon; Monday to Friday, 1:00 PM to 8:00 PM; Saturday, 1:00 PM to 5:00 PM.

Music Archives from the fourteenth to the nineteenth centuries; about 16,000 records here.

Mechelen is the international center for carillonneurs, who carry on the great tradition of Jef Denijn (1862-1941). In the last two decades of the nineteenth century, Denijn revived interest in the bellringer's technique. Staf Nees continued work in the school founded by Denijn (see *Conservatories*), and in Mechelen today, you will find the Beiaard Museum, the only carillon museum in the world. (*Beiaard* is the Flemish word for carillon.)

Conservatories and Schools

There are six schools in Belgium with the designation Conservatoire Royal or its Flemish equivalent, Koninklijk Muziekconservatorium: two in Brussels, and one each in Liège, Mons, Ghent, and Antwerp. This title is given only to state institutions supported by subsidies from their provinces and towns. All of these are supposedly equally prestigious, although the two in Brussels are best known. The Ministries of Culture (French and Flemish) sponsor them. Preparation for admission to these conservatories is undertaken at an école, académie, or conservatoire communal (the most advanced of the three types of institutions just mentioned).

There is no instrumental music program in Belgian grade schools, but they do have an extensive system of musical schools in all communities. Classes are held Sunday mornings and afternoons when school is out, and both adults and children attend. Gifted children continue later at one of the royal conservatories. Every one of the nineteen communes (boroughs) of Brussels has one école or academy—and sometimes two, for linguistic reasons.

At the universities of Ghent, Liége, Brussels, and Leuven there are departments or seminars in musicology.

Berchem (Antwerp)

Académie de Musique
114 avenue du Roi-Albert   Tel: 30 26 60

Brugge

Stedelijk Muziekconservatorium (see Libraries)
23 St. Jacobstraat   Tel: 33 43 91

Charleroi

Conservatoire de Musique   Tel: 31 05 37
Rue Biarant

Ghent

Koninklijk Muziekconservatorium (see Libraries)
50 Hoogpoort   Tel: 25 15 15

Seminaire voor Muziekgeschiedenis (Institute of Musicology)
Rijksuniversiteit Ghent
2 Blandijnberg   Tel: 23 38 21

Kortrijk

Stedelijk Muziekconservatorium
7 Begijnhofstraat   Tel: 22 27 06

Liège

Institut de Musicologie (see Libraries)
1 place Cockerill

Conservatoire Royal de Musique (see Libraries)
14 rue Forgeur

Mechelen (Malines)

École des Carillonneurs
Sint Janstraat and Merodestraat

Stedelijk Muziekconservatorium
16 Wollemarkt   Tel: 21 35 52

Mons

Conservatoire Royal de Musique
7 rue de Nimy   Tel: 33 27 28

Tournai

Conservatoire de Musique
64 rue Saint-Martin   Tel: 22 39 15

Verviers

Conservatoire de Musique
6 rue Chapuis   Tel: 33 52 52

Waterloo

Chapelle Musicale Reine Elisabeth
Post graduate, three-year course for violinists, cellists, pianists, and composers. An entrance exam is given every three years to qualified applicants. Those who succeed in gaining admission have all living expenses and tuition paid for from a fund established by Queen Elisabeth.

Musical Landmarks

Damme

Richard Strauss's tone poem *Till Eulenspiegel* derives from the legend of Tyl used by Charles Coster in his book *Legends of the Glorious Adventures of Tyl Ulenspiegel.* Coster (1827–1879) set the scene of his book in Damme, Belgium.

Ghent

Maurice Maeterlinck (1862–1949), a Gantois whose play *Pelléas et Mélisande* inspired **Debussy, Fauré,** and **Schoenberg,** was the first Belgian to receive the Nobel prize, in 1911.

Liège

At the Conservatoire Royale de Liège, 14 rue Forgeur, a museum has been established in memory of the composer-violinist **Eugène Ysaÿe** (1858–1931). Ysaÿe's son is still actively involved with this memorial to his father. Ysaÿe's grave is in the cemetery at Ixelles near Brussels.

Scores and manuscripts of the composer and organist **Pierre Froidebise** (1914–1962) are preserved at his home, 111 rue de Laveu, Liège.

Saint-Amand

Émile Verhaeren (1855–1916) (see *Brussels, Miscellaneous*) was born in this little village and lies buried in a majestic mausoleum built into the river.

Stavelot

Guillaume Apollinaire (1880–1918), whose text *Les Mamelles de Tirésias* was set by **Poulenc,** spent time in a pension here.

Miscellaneous

Carillons

In this country of carillonneurs, here is a word about carillon concerts. The main concerts given by carillonneurs are in the following cities:

Antwerp

Our Lady Cathedral, Fridays, 11:30 AM to 12:30 PM, June to September; also Monday, 9:00 PM to 10:00 PM in St. Catherine's Church; Wednesday, 8:30 PM to 9:30 PM.

Bruges

Belfry, mid-June to end of September, Monday, Wednesday, and Saturday from 9:00 PM to 10:00 PM; Sunday, from 11:45 AM to 12:30 PM. From October to mid-June, Sunday, Wednesday, and Saturday, from 11:45 AM to 12:30 PM.

Ghent

Belfry, during the summer months, at main festivals and holidays.

Mechelen

St. Rombouts Cathedral, mid-June to end of August, on Monday, at 8:30 PM. (See p. 31 for mention of world-famous school for carillonneurs here.)

Other towns include: Aalst, Charleroi, Dendermonde, Diest, Diksmuide, Florenville (forty-eight chimes), Huy, Ieper, Kortrijk, Leuwen, Liège, Lier, Malmédy, Mons, Nieuwpoort, Oudenaarde, Tongeren, Tournai, and Turnhout.

Most carillons play automatically on the hour and half-hour; some on the quarter-hour too.

Musical Organizations

Charleroi

Association des Concerts du Conservatoire de Charleroi
Rue Biarant

Kortrijk (Courtrai)

Stedelijke Discotheek
Guido Gezellestraat

Liège

Collegium novarum de Liège
15 rue Haute-Sauverniere
M. André Noiret

Association des Concerts Permanents
170 rue Fond-Pirette

Société Liègeoise de Musicologie
Soc. libre d'Émulation
Place du Vingt Août

Musée Grétry
14 rue Forgeur
Curator: M. Radoux-Rogier

Mechelen

De Vrienden van het Conservatorium
67 Stuyvenbergstraat

Mons

Association des Concerts du Conservatoire de Mons
7 rue de Nimy

Fonds Musicologique de la Cathédrale St. Wandru

Schoten-Koningshof

Vereniging voor Muziekgeschiedenis te Antwerpen
"Ruysdael"

Verviers

Fonds Guillaume Lekeu
Administration Communale

Waterloo

Chapelle Musicale de la Reine Elisabeth
Argenteuil

SYMPHONY ORCHESTRAS

Brugge

Orkest van het Muziekconservatorium
57 Peperstraat

Charleroi

Orchestre Symphonique du Conservatoire de Charleroi

Ghent

Orkest van het Koninklijk Muziekconservatorium
50 Hoogpoort

Kortrijk

Orkest van het Muziekconservatorium
18 Bredastraat

Liège

Orchestre de la Ville de Liège
14 rue Forgeur

Orchestre du Conservatoire de Musique
14 rue Forgeur

Louvain

Orkest van het Muziekconservatorium
24 Blijde Inkomstraat

Mechelen

Orkest van het Muziekconservatorium
16 Wollemarkt

Mons

Orchestre du Conservatoire Royal de Musique
7 rue de Nimy

Namur

Orchestre du Conservatoire de Musique
121 chaussée de Louvain

Oostende

Orkest van het Muziekconservatorium
36 Romestraat

OPERA COMPANIES

Ghent

Koninklijke Opera Ghent
3 Schouwburgstraat

Liège

Théâtre Royal de Liège
2 rue des Dominicains

Mons

Théâtre Royal de Mons

Verviers

Grand Théâtre de Verviers
2 rue des Artistes

The Business of Music

MUSIC PUBLISHERS

Ghent

Cnudde
    7 Voldersstraat, 9000 Ghent

Liège

Muraille
    30 rue des Augustins, 4000 Liège

Tyssens, E.
    30 rue des Clarisses, 4000 Liège

Mechelen

Musica Sacra
    72 Koningin Astridlaan, 2800 Mechelen

De Monte
    9 Adeghem, 2800 Mechelen

Dessain, H.
    9 Bleekstraat, 2800 Mechelen

Oostende

Andel
    26 Madeliefjesstraat, 8400 Oostende

Tournai

Delmotte, M.
    24–28 chaussée de Lille, 7599 Tournai

INSTRUMENT MAKERS: ORGAN

Duffel

Stevens, J.
32 Leopoldstraat, 2570 Duffel

Herselt

Bels-Houdt, Bernard
3170 Herselt

Menen

Anneessens, P.
10–12 rue des Bénédictines, 8600 Menen

INSTRUMENT MAKERS: HARPSICHORD

Desselgem

Maine, W.
13 Ooigemstraat, 8748 Desselgem

INSTRUMENT MAKERS: LUTE

Liège

M. Lanolette
39 rue Reynies, Liège   Tel: (041) 23 11 76

Verviers

Jo Blavier
42 rue du Gymnase, Verviers   Tel: (087) 33 74 54

INSTRUMENT MAKERS: GENERAL

Liège

Palais de la Musique
50 place St. Severin, Liège   Tel: (041) 23 11 23

Festivals

There are two principal festivals occurring annually in Belgium: the Festival of Flanders and the Festival de Wallonie. Participating cities are fairly numerous, and we have therefore listed them alphabetically, including addresses where known. In some instances, specific concert halls or castles where performances take place are also cited. A third, much smaller festival, the Festival International du Hainaut, is also listed for your convenience.

Festival van Vlaanderen (Festival of Flanders)

Antwerp (Anvers)

Stadhuis
Dates: the month of September.
The Royal Flemish Opera (KVO), the concert hall *(Dierentuinzaal)* of the Zoological Society of Antwerp, and the Rubenshuis (see above under *Antwerp* for more information) hold concert, opera, and other musical performances.

Brugge (Bruges)

Gistelse Steenweg
The Journées Musicales Internationales de Bruges and the Concours International d'Orgue (organ competition) take place here the first two weeks in August.
    The Journées feature different instruments and different composers each year. The concerts are given in the historic buildings of Bruges like the Town Hall, the Memling Museum, the Cathedral, and the various churches.

Brussels

BRT, 52 boulevard Reyers   Tel: (02) 49 67 82
This is the principal address for information. Another address is listed under Ghent, the Flemish city which is headquarters for the area.
Dates: Spring Festival is April 21 to July 5. Summer Festival is August 1 to
    September 20.

The Cathédrale St. Michel and the Palais des Beaux-Arts are also the scene of various performances during August and September. About 140 different performances are given throughout the country.

Ghent (Gand)

26 Sint-Margrietstraat   Tel: (09) 25 97 40
Dates: From about August 15 to September 15.
Box Office: open 10:00 AM to noon, 2:00 PM to 5:00 PM daily except Saturday and
    Sunday.
Customary Dress: evening dress is often worn at these presentations.

Kortrijk (Courtrai)

Koorfestival, 12 Jan Breydellaan.
Dates: the months of April and May.
International Choral Festival. Concerts are given in the completely renovated Town Theater, in the special setting of the gothic chamber of the Town Hall, and in the lovely Church of Our Lady.

Leuwen (Louvain)

Dates: August and September.
Sint-Pieterskerk (St. Peter's Church), the Stadhuis (Town Hall), the Stadsschouwburg (Municipal Theater), and the Universiteitsaula (auditorium of the University) all have performances.

Mechelen (Malines)

Dienst voor Toerisme, Stadhuis (Town Hall)   Tel: (015) 21 30 37
Dates: late August to late September.
Choirs, chamber music, organ, and carillon recitals in the Mechelen International Music Days.
   The musical events at Mechelen are grouped around different themes (e.g., the organ and its exponents, carillon concerts).

Tongeren

Basilica Concerten, 15 Kielenstraat
Concerts are given in the Basilica here during June.

To summarize, the Festival of Flanders takes place in about thirty medieval halls, castles, and cathedrals of the old capitals of Flanders. Symphonic and chamber music, operas, oratorios, and recitals are presented during the Festival. Ask your travel agent in advance regarding ticket information; also the Belgian Tourist Bureau's Office of Information at 720 Fifth Avenue, New York, N.Y. 10019 (212-582-1750) willingly offers assistance. In Belgium itself, the best organization to contact is the CeBeDeM (see entry above) in Brussels.

Festival de Wallonie

Athus

Dates: September to October.
Automne Musical d'Athus.

Chimay

c/o M.P. Fromont, 129 avenue du Pesage, 1050 Brussels
Dates: mid-June to mid-July.
Festival de Chimay; chamber music.

Recitals and concerts of chamber music will be given in the elegant rococo-style theater, where many well-known artists gave performances, including Bériot, Aubert, and Malibran.

Dinant

Date: July.
Juillet Musical de Dinant; chamber music, vocal music.

Liège

c/o Mlle. Suzanne Clercx, 16 place du XX Août
Dates: September.
Festival de Liège, "Les Nuits de Septembre" orchestral, operatic, and chamber music concerts.

This festival has been canceled for the last several years.

Mouscron

Dates: mid-April to mid-May.
Printemps Musical de Mouscron; chamber music and ballet.

Saint-Hubert

c/o M. Pierart, Palais Abbatial, 6900 Saint Hubert   Tel: (06) 16 14 05
Dates: the month of July, on Saturdays, Sundays and Wednesdays.
International Music Festival of Saint-Hubert.

This small, picturesque Ardennes town is a very active cultural center, which organizes an important international music festival. The concerts are given in the Abbatial Palace and in the Basilica of Saint-Hubert, the churches of Nassogne, Waha, Montleban, and Neufschâteau.

Stavelot

c/o M. R. Micha, 11 allée Verte, 4970 Stavelot   Tel: (080) 88 24 50
Dates: the month of August.
Festival de Stavelot.

This festival puts the accent on chamber music in particular. Its main aim is to familiarize the public with music. The former Benedictine abbey and its eighteenth-century hall serve as the setting for the Festival, as does the church of Stavelot when larger ensembles are performing. Guest orchestras and soloists perform.

Val-Dieu

Dates: mid-April to mid-May.
Concerts de Printemps à l'Abbaye du Val-Dieu; chamber music.

Festival International du Hainaut
c/o M.C. Halsberghe, Jardin du Mayeur, 7000 Mons
Dates: from September through November.
Concerts of symphonic music are given in the towns of Mons, Tournai, and Charleroi.

Smaller Festivals

Blankenberge

Municipality
c/o Mr. Stubbe, 8370 Blankenberge   Tel: (050) 41 24 45
Dates: July and August.
Organ, violin, and piano recitals. Not only classical music is presented; sometimes jazz concerts are given.

Heusy

Lyric Season
Mr. G. Demoulin, 111 avenue Reine Astrid, 4802 Heusy   Tel: (087) 22 52 63
Dates: mid-July through August.
Operas and operettas are presented at the Casino Theater.

Huy

Festival de Huy
c/o M. Jean Duchesne, Hôtel de Ville, 5200 Huy   Tel: (085) 21 78 21
Dates: April and May.

Namur

Namur Festival
c/o M. R. Rombaert, 1 rue Baron de Moreau, 5000 Namur
Dates: June to mid-September.
Symphonic music; special concerts are given in various châteaux within the province of Namur.

Neerpelt

European Festival of Music for Youth
Secretariaat voor het festival, 25 Stationstraat, 3580 Neerpelt
Tel: (01) 14 20 52
Dates: four days at the end of April.
This is a European music festival in the north of Limburg, designed for young people. More than one hundred choirs give performances in three halls. Young people attend from Czechoslovakia, France, Germany, Great Britain, Ireland, Italy, Luxembourg, the Netherlands, Norway, Poland, Switzerland, and Yugoslavia.

Oostende (Ostend)

North Sea Festival
Casino-Kursaal van Oostende, 8400 Oostende   Tel: (059) 70 51 11
Dates: July and August.
Concerts, ballet, variety entertainment, soloists and ensembles.
This festival is held in the auditorium of the Casino-Kursaal.

Spa

International Festival of French Songs
ASBL, "Les Festivals de Spa," Hôtel de Ville, 4880 Spa
Dates: first week in July.
Belgian, Canadian, French, and Swiss singers perform in the Casino.

Competitions

Bruges

International Organ, Harpsichord, and Recorder Competition
Secretariat of the International Fortnight of Music
30 Collaert Mansionstraat
Dates: annually in July.
Deadline: June; for those under 36 years of age.
Awards: Bfr 40,000, 30,000, 20,000 and 10,000.
The category of recorder was added for the first time in 1972.

Brussels

Queen Elisabeth of Belgium International Music Competition
(Concours Musical International Reine Elisabeth)
11 rue Baron Horta
Dates: annually toward the end of April, continuing for about four weeks.
Age Limit: 17 to 31.
Awards: first prize of Bfr 200,000; second through twelfth prizes, Bfr 150,000 to
   Bfr 20,000; also medals. Additional prizes of Bfr 10,000 are awarded to
   each of the twelve competitors of the second stage tests who were not
   selected for the final test.
Deadline: January 15.
This contest was inaugurated in 1937 in memory of Eugene Ysaÿe (see p. 33).
The winners of the first two years included David Oistrakh and Emil Gilels,
both unknown at the time. Later winners from various countries were Leonid
Kogan (also Russian), Leon Fleischer (American), Vladimir Ashkenazy (Russian), Jaime Laredo (South American), Philippe Entremont (French), John
Browning (English), and Joseph Silverstein (American). The contest alternates
between instrumentalists (violin and piano), and composers, with a complete
cycle every *four* years. (One year there is no competition.)
   The order of the contestants is fixed by drawing lots. There are several
stages to the auditions: semifinalist and, later, finalist eliminations, all of which
take place in public. All pieces are played from memory. One brand-new
concerto, unknown to the twelve finalists, is composed for the occasion by a
leading Belgian composer, selected by the jury, and given to the contestants to
learn and to practice one week before the finals. The compositions selected
usually alternate between French and Flemish.

International Voice Competition (Concours International de Chant de
Belgique)
39 rue Fritz-Toussaint, c/o Les Amis de Mozart
Dates: usually in May in those years when there is no Queen Elisabeth contest;
   otherwise in August.
Age Limit: 20 to 35.
Deadline: February 1.
Contestants should have mastered representative selections from the concert
and operatic repertory, have an endorsement from their school or teacher, have
proof of age, nationality, and residence.

Liège

International Bel Canto Competition
5 quai du Condroz

Dates: not fixed.
Age Limit: 20 to 35.
Awards: total over Bfr 30,000.
Deadline: September 1.

Les Amis de l'Art Lyrique
Siège Social, 10 rue des Dominicains
Dates: September.
Deadline: August 15.

Liège Competition for String Quartets (Concours International de Quatuor à Cordes)
Secrétariat du Concours, 66 rue de Joie, 4000 Liège   Tel: 52 65 70; 52 82 12
Dates: about two weeks in middle of September.
Age Limit: none.
Awards: first prizes in each category. For composition, Bfr 40,000; for performance, Bfr 70,000; for construction of the instruments, Bfr 125,000. Other prizes (see below).
Deadline: June 30.
This contest is unusual because it is in three parts: Composition, Performance, and Construction of the instruments. Details for each category are explained in a brochure obtainable on request from the above address. In the composition contest a total of Bfr 175,000 is divided among three winners. Again, there are semifinalists and finalists, both of whom appear in public performances.

Contestants in the performance category are welcomed from all nations. Five specific works are performed and the jury divides a total of Bfr 140,000 between two winners, two quartets.

For makers of stringed instruments, the prize is again Bfr 175,000. Instruments are judged on the basis of their workmanship as well as their sonority.

Verviers

Echo des Travailleurs International (International Competition for Solo Voice)
Secrétariat, 6 rue de Gymnase
Dates: Biennially, 1975, 1977, etc.
Age limit: under 35 years of age.
Awards: first prize of Bfr 40,000. Fourteen additional prizes totaling Bfr 136,000. Diplomas.
Open to professional and amateur singers.
Deadline: in March.

Periodicals

A la Philharmonique

Société Philharmonique de Bruxelles, 11 rue Baron Horta, Brussels 1
Semimonthly; free

Ad te Levavi (Journal of Serious Music)

19 Minderbroedersstraat, Hasselt
Bimonthly

Adem (Journal of Liturgical Music)

Lemmensinstituut, 51 Herestraat, Leuven
Bimonthly

Agenda des Jeunesses Musicales de Belgique

Palais des Beaux Arts, Brussels 1
6 issues yearly
Flemish edition entitled *Tijdschrift van Jeugd en Muziek van België*

L'Agenda Musical (Concert Guide of the Philharmonic of Brussels)

Palais des Beaux Arts, Brussels
Monthly

Ars Musica (Bulletin of the Association of Students and Former Students of the Royal Conservatory of Music in Brussels)

30 rue de la Régence, Brussels
Six issues yearly; also published in Flemish

Basilica (Concert Bulletin)

c/o "Nieuws uit Limburg," Tongeren

Beaux Arts

10 rue Royale, Brussels

Het Belgisch Muziekleven

5 Wolstraat, 1000 Brussels
Bimonthly

Bulletin de la SABAM (Belgian Society of Composers, Arrangers, and Editors of Music)

4 boulevard de l'Empéreur, 1000 Brussels
Monthly
Flemish equivalent: *Tijdschrift van SABAM*

Bulletin d'Information de la Vie Musicale Belge

Conseil National de la Musique, 5 rue aux Laines, Brussels 1
Bimonthly
Flemish equivalent: *Tijdschrift van het Belgisch Musikleven*

Caecilia (Official Bulletin of the Belgian Music Federation)

18 rue Auguste Orts, Brussels 1
Quarterly; Flemish edition has the same name

Clés Pour la Musique (Published by the Belgian Broadcasting System, R.T.B.)

10 rue Royal, 1000 Brussels
Published on the 1st, 10th, and 20th of each month

Comoedia (Covers performances of opera, concerts, and theater)

25 Boomgaardstraat, Antwerp
Weekly

Danse, Musique, Théâtre en Belgique

Arto, 22 boulevard Maurice Lemonnier, Brussels 1
Annually

De Praestant (Organ Music)

26 Abdijstraat, Tongerloo
Quarterly

De Scene (Sponsored by Kultuurraad voor Vlaanderen; contains commentaries and reviews on plays and performances in Amsterdam; written in Dutch)

Theatercentrum, 28 Jan van Rijswijklaan, Antwerp
Monthly

L'Éventail (Published by the Théâtre Royal de la Monnaie)

4 rue Léopold, Brussels 1
Monthly

Fondation Eugène Ysaÿe Bulletin d'Information (editions in English and French)

39 rue de l'Escrime, Brussels 19
Three issues yearly

Gewijde Dienst (Church and Organ Music of Flanders)

c/o Sacrista, 27 Ardociesteenweg, Roeselare
Bimonthly

Information—Jeunesses Musicales

5 rue Baron Horta, Brussels 1
Monthly

Jonge Muziek (Music in the Schools)

33 Van Putlei, Antwerp
Quarterly

Le Journal des Beaux Arts

12 rue Baron Horta, Brussels 1
Weekly

Juke Box

Juke Box N.V., 37 Stuivenberg, Malines
Monthly

Kunst en Cultuur (Published by the Palais des Beaux Arts)

10 Koningstraat, Brussels
Bimonthly

Het Madrigaal (Choral Singing and Madrigals)

Te Hoogstraten, Antwerp
Quarterly

Mededelingen (Society for Music History of Antwerp)

76 Belpairestraat, Berchem-Antwerp

Music

13 rue de la Madeleine, Brussels
Twice monthly
Published in English, French and Dutch

Musica Sacra

Interdiocesane Kerkmuziekschool
70 Koningin Astridlaan, Mechelen
Quarterly

Muziekopvoeding (Music Educators' Journal)

13 Onder der Toren, Mechelen
Three times yearly

Platen Kiezen (Independent Journal for Records and Musical Hi-Fidelity)

13 Guldenspoorstraat, Ghent
Monthly

Revue Belge de Musicologie

Société Belge de Musicologie, 30 rue de la Régence, 1000 Brussels
Quarterly
Flemish edition: *Belgisch Tijdschrift voor Muziekwetenschap*

La Revue des Disques et de la Haute Fidélité

Editions Dereume, 69 rue du Marché, 1000 Brussels
Ten issues yearly

La Revue de Son

36 rue Philippe de Champagne, Brussels 1
Monthly (Ten issues a year)

Revue International de Musique

38 rue Émile Lecomte, Brussels 18
Quarterly

Rhythms, Blues (Jazz)

143 rue de Theux, Brussels 4

Tijdschrift voor de Beoefenaars van Volksdans, Volkszang, Huismuziek

(V.D.C.V., a review for performers of folk dances, folk song, and lighter
music)

23 Oude Donklaan, Deurne-Antwerp
Quarterly

La Vie Musicale Belge (Newsletter of Musical Life in Belgium)

Conseil National de la Musique, 11 rue Baron Horta, Brussels 1
Quarterly

Vivaldiana

Centre International de Documentation Antonio Vivaldi
32 rue Berckmans, Brussels 6
Irregular

Vlaams Muziektijdschrift (Formerly entitled *Harop*. Sponsored by Ministerie van
   Nederlandse Cultuur; features book and record reviews, articles on Flemish
   composers and musical life in general.)

Algemeen Nederlands Zangverbond, 22–24 Oudaan, Antwerp
Ten issues yearly

Vlaanderen (Journal of Art and Culture)

Christelijk Vlaams Kunstenaarsverbond, 12 Pontonstraat, Oostende
Bimonthly

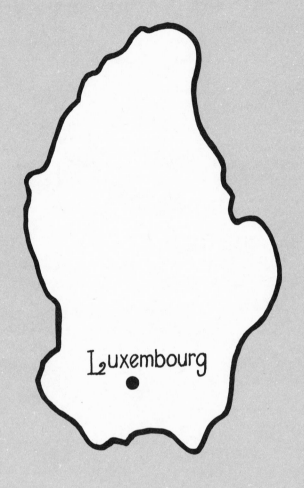

Luxembourg

Luxembourg

ꝏLuxembourg

LUXEMBOURG CITY   Tel. prefix: none

Guides and Services

Office National du Tourisme
Place de la Gare, Luxembourg City   Tel: 48 79 99; 48 11 99
This office is located at the air terminal, near the main rail station. For those
who want to write ahead, the address is P. O. Box 1001, Luxembourg.

Luxembourg National Tourist Office (USA)
1 Dag Hammarskjold Plaza, New York, N.Y. 10017   Tel: (212) 751-9650

Tourist Information (in English)
This annual guide to Luxembourg offers information on hotels, restaurants,
sports facilities, places of interest, museums, cultural events, etc. It is available
at both offices cited above.

NATIONAL HOLIDAYS

January	1	New Year's Day
February	*	Shrove Monday and Tuesday
April	*	Easter Monday
May	1	Labor Day
	*	Ascension Day
	*	Whit Monday
June	23	Grand Duke's Birthday
August	15	Assumption Day
November	1	All Saints' Day
	2	All Souls' Day

December	24	Christmas Eve (half-day)
	25	Christmas
	27	St. Stephen's Day

* = movable

Opera Houses and Concert Halls

The Duchy of Luxembourg, hardly large enough to possess a concert hall or opera house, offers its citizens operatic and concert performances in the Nouveau Théâtre Municipal.

Nouveau Théâtre Municipal
Ville de Luxembourg
Season: January through May, presenting opera, concerts, ballet, chamber music, and theatrical performances.
Box Office Hours: daily from 4:00 PM to 7:00 PM   Tel: 47 08 95
In addition, every Thursday from January through March, a concert by the Symphony Orchestra of Radio Luxembourg is given in the auditorium of the Villa Louvigny in the city of Luxembourg.

Libraries and Museums

Bibliothèque Nationale [Ben. 1]
14a boulevard Royal
Hours: Monday to Friday, 9:00 AM to 6:00 PM. Closed during August.

Conservatoire de Musique de la Ville de Luxembourg, Bibliothèque [Ben. 2]
16 rue de St. Esprit
Hours: Monday to Friday, 8:00 AM to noon and 2:00 PM to 6:00 PM. Closed July 1 to October 1.

Conservatories and Schools

Conservatoire de Musique de la Ville de Luxembourg
14-16 rue du St. Esprit   Tel: 96 29 50; 96 29 51

Conservatoire de Musique d'Esch-sur-Alzette, Luxembourg
10 rue de l'Église, Esch-sur-Alzette   Tel: 5 21 01

Festivals

International Open Air Festival of Music and Drama
Mailing Address: Wiltz, Grand Duchy of Luxembourg   Tel: 9 61 99; 61 45
Season: about two weeks in late July and early August; offers opera, drama, ballet, concerts at the Château.
Box Office: Bureau du Festival (Château), Wiltz.
Hours: 10:00 AM to 11:30 AM and 5:00 PM to 6:00 PM daily.
Authorized Ticket Agency: Bureau d'Accueil, Office Nationale du Tourisme, place de la Gare, Luxembourg Ville.
Seating Capacity: 2100.
Housing accommodations are available through the Syndicat d'initiative (at the Château) at Wiltz, or any tourist office. (The term, "Syndicat d'initiative," is regularly used in French-speaking countries; it means the "Office of Information.")

Haarlem

Bussum

Zwolle

Amsterdam

Hilversum

Leiden

Breukelen

Bilthoven

Wassenaar

Utrecht

The Hague

Rotterdam

's-Hertogenbosch

Kerkrade

Maastricht

Holland

✻Holland

At different times during the last six hundred years, Holland (or the Netherlands, as its citizens prefer to call it) has been a part of France, Burgundy, the Holy Roman Empire, and Spain. For a very short time, Belgium, in its turn, belonged to the Netherlands, and for this reason many nineteenth-century historians describe the musical heritage of the Netherlands as encompassing the music of both the northern Protestant Dutch, and their southern neighbors, the Belgian Catholics.

Extant manuscripts from the fourteenth century reveal the existence of monophonic songs in the Dutch language, but among the fifteenth-century group of Netherlands composers, only Jacob Obrecht can really be considered a Dutchman. The second important Dutch composer and teacher is Sweelinck (1562–1621), who wrote all his instrumental works for keyboard instruments. Sweelinck became famous for his organ playing at the Oudekerk (Old Church) in Amsterdam; and because his pupils included nearly all the leading German organists and organ composers of the early Baroque, he was called *Der deutsche Organistenmacher,* the maker of German organists. Many programs of Dutch artists today reflect this interest in organ music.

In the seventeenth and eighteenth centuries, Dutch music was first under the influence of the Italians and later of the French. During the nineteenth century, the two composers whose personalities made the strongest impression on the Dutch were Mendelssohn and Schumann. Later, as a result of the rising tide of nationalism, a revival of interest in Dutch literature, architecture, painting, and, finally, music took place in the 1880s. In 1888 the Amsterdam Concertgebouw Orchestra was organized. Under Willem Mengelberg, their conductor for almost fifty years, they achieved international renown.

The first prominent Dutch composer of the modern era is Alphons Diepenbrock (1862–1921), whose compositions show the influence of the Austrian Gustav Mahler (1860–1911), and the French Impressionist Claude Debussy (1862–1918). Apparently the next generation also revealed their debt to these two masters. Active both as a teacher and a composer was Sem Dresden

(1881-1957), first Director of the Amsterdam Conservatory from 1924 to 1937 and later (until 1949), Director of the Royal Conservatory in The Hague. Dresden was also behind the efforts to reprint the complete works of earlier Dutch masters. In this endeavor he had the assistance of several fine musicologists, including the eminent Professor Albert Smijers.

Probably the most significant figure in Dutch music of the twentieth century is Willem Pijper (1894-1947), whose compositions and whose pupils put Dutch music on the map. His early compositions reflect the influence of the German and French schools, but eventually Pijper's works show a distinct personality of their own. Henk Badings (b. 1907), who studied for a short time with Pijper, and Ton de Leeuw (b. 1926), who apprenticed with Messaien in Paris, are other well-known composers.

The intensely sincere interest and support of musical culture in contemporary Holland finds few parallels in other countries. In addition to schools in Amsterdam, The Hague, and Rotterdam, other cities like Groningen, Tilburg, and Maastricht also have conservatories. Musicology may be studied at the universities of Amsterdam, Leyden, and Utrecht where it forms part of the Faculty of Letters and Philosophy.

Church musicians and carillonists can receive special training in their own schools. In fact, competitions specifically for organists and carillonists are held annually in Holland. Numerous state scholarships are awarded to music students, and the state inspects and checks on standards in all these schools. Books, films, and recordings distributed by a considerable number of music dealers and publishers further confirm the importance of music in Dutch cultural life.

Apart from three important radio orchestras, Holland has eleven symphony orchestras (for which the government usually covers fifty percent of salaries as well as social contributions of members), and about 110 amateur symphony orchestras involving approximately 7,000 working members from all levels of the population.* These figures are particularly impressive when we recall that the total population of the country is a mere 13,200,000 and that thirty-seven percent of the Dutch live on only five percent of the land area. Cramped quarters are among the inescapable facts of Dutch existence. So is musicmaking!

---

*Fontes (1974) No.3, the journal of the International Association of Music Libraries reports (in an issue devoted to Holland) that the Dutch now have twenty professional orchestras, sixteen conservatories and music schools, one hundred and fifty music schools for amateurs, three thousand amateur choirs, five thousand Roman Catholic church choirs, one hundred amateur orchestras, two thousand military and brass bands, thirty-two hundred drum bands, and countless amateur "soloists"! Readers might also be interested in the special 1969 Netherlands issue of the *Journal of the British Institute of Recorded Sound* (No. 36).

Musical events are to be found every month of the year in Holland. For over twenty-five years, the summer Holland Festival has been one of the most attractive in all Europe. Basically by and for the Dutch, it is, as the English critic David Stevens has said, "open to the present and the future without forgetting the past." By now, free concerts and theater in the streets and other public places are expected contributions from the Festival's directors. Concerts will range from jazz—incidentally, Amsterdam is one of the centers for jazz and its aficionados—to programs marking the anniversaries of Josquin Des Prez and Sweelinck, as well as to works by twentieth-century composers like Willem Pijper and his disciples.

The Holland Festival differs from those in other countries in that it is not restricted to one city; it is not limited to a few days or two weeks; it is not devoted to the works of one great master like Bach or Wagner or even to a few Dutch composers. Although the programs vary each year, this festival always includes the participation of every city, town, and hamlet in Holland; it continues throughout the summer months; it offers the music of composers of international as well as national renown; it presents works written for many different media over a period of several centuries. In 1968, for example, the Festival focused on the works of the Viennese School of Schoenberg, Berg, and Webern. Other composers' works were performed, but the emphasis was on these three. In order to highlight the works of these relatively inaccessible moderns, several special brochures were printed to help familiarize the Dutch with the necessary background for an understanding of this music. Most musicians agree that the Dutch include some of the most sympathetic of contemporary audiences.

We must not forget another fact of Dutch history that affected musical life in the country. Because the Netherlands at one time had numerous possessions in southeast Asia, we can find several collections of non-Western musical instruments in different Dutch museums. The items were brought back to Europe by visiting scholars and collectors.

Among the best-known music information centers in Europe is the Dutch foundation called Donemus, whose aim is to promote the knowledge of contemporary Dutch music in the Netherlands as well as throughout the world. Radio Nederland Wereldomroep, in Hilversum, publishes a pamphlet by Dr. Jos Wouters entitled *Five Centuries of Dutch Music* which should be consulted by those interested in a quick review of the subject.

The Dutch are not famous for their sense of humor. They do compensate for this lack with a remarkable sense of justice in their administration of cultural projects. They believe that audiences have the right to enjoy the best in musicmaking. To assure themselves of fine conservatories, orchestras, soloists, etc., the government offers subsidies and support to music and musicians. On the other hand, the artists have the legal assurance of the state, which both protects them against competition from dilettantes—only qualified artists receive support—and also continuously promotes interest in music, thus assuring the artists of a constantly growing public for their works.

Guides and Services

Tourist Office (V.V.V., which stands for Vereniging Voor Vreemdelingenver-keer)
3 Hofweg, The Hague   Tel: (070) 11 62 60

Netherlands National Tourist Office
17 Mauritskade, The Hague   Tel: (070) 18 33 00

Netherlands National Tourist Office (USA)
576 Fifth Avenue, New York, N.Y. 10036   Tel: (212) 245-5320

Netherlands National Tourist Office (USA)
681 Market Street, Room 941, San Francisco, California 94105
                                                         Tel: (415) 781-3387

Holland (in English)
Appears twice a year (March-August, September-February) and includes a diary of events taking place in Holland throughout the year. Musical events are listed with all others.

Holland—Playground of Europe (in English)
Provides a selection of tourist and cultural attractions. It is less comprehensive than the booklet mentioned above. Both available at addresses listed above.

NATIONAL HOLIDAYS

January	1	New Year's Day
March	*	Good Friday
April	*	Easter Monday
	30	Queen's Birthday
May	*	Ascension Day
	*	Whit Monday
December	25	Christmas

* = movable

AMSTERDAM

With close to one million inhabitants, Amsterdam is not only the largest city in Holland, it is also virtually the capital of the country. The ground plan of the city has not changed much since the Middle Ages, when Amsterdam first appeared as a settlement on the Amstel River. The city has never forgotten its river—Amsterdam is known as "the Venice of the North"—and is built around a series of concentric canals. Despite this physical situation, which one might expect to delay its commerce and industry, Amsterdam has grown phenomenally in recent years. Today it is regarded as one of Europe's centers of art and culture.

An unforgettable feature of this modern city is its multitude of cyclists. Young and old, rich and poor, farmer and financier, all use their bicycles as a means of transportation at some time during the week. The Dutchman is never in a hurry. Steadfast and constantly on the move, he has a passion for punctuality and is never late.

Permanent rivalry exists among the three largest Dutch cities. The natives of Amsterdam look down on the citizens of The Hague and vice versa. Rotterdam thinks of itself as a second New York, while Amsterdam imagines it is another Paris. But these cosmopolitan aspirations are balanced by good taste. Any display of wealth is scorned. Nothing in the external appearance of a rich citizen distinguishes him from a small tradesman or an artisan.

Owing to their lack of a landed gentry whose personal musicians supplied music for entertainment, the Dutch grew accustomed to making music at home. Of all the arts, certainly music is the favorite. Most children in Amsterdam have music lessons and many a family plays chamber music. Listening to the radio is another favorite pastime. Music is everybody's concern. A visitor in Amsterdam can find out the program of the Concertgebouw simply by inquiring at the concierge's desk in any hotel. Curiously, the theater is less popular here.

The people of Amsterdam have responded warmly to foreign musicians for more than a century. Schumann, for example, always enjoyed his visits to this country. To this day, the most favorable terms available to performing musicians come through concert managers in Amsterdam. The city is alive, tingling with excitement, responsive to the new in music and in art, as well as social mores. Jazz musicians find this a highly desirable place in which to hold their concerts, as do the electronic and avant-garde classical musicians.

One unusual feature of musical life here is the extent to which religion permeates every facet of a musician's experience. The Dutch are divided into Catholics, Protestants, and others—each completely separate from his neighbor. To be Catholic in Holland means buying produce from a Catholic farmer, voting for the Catholic party, employing Catholic servants, and having Catholic friends (See Anthony Bailey's *The Light in Holland*). For musicians it means joining Catholic professional and fraternal organizations. And for every Catholic association, there must be a Protestant equivalent. Catholics have their own radio stations, newspapers, clubs, and universities. The Dutch broadcasting system, though state-owned, is divided into five groups: liberal Protestant, orthodox Protestant, Catholic, neutral and liberal, and labor. Organists are grouped by religion, as are all instrumentalists (see *Musical Organizations* below).

The headquarters of many principal musical organizations are in Amsterdam. It is the hub of the nation. If you have time for only one Dutch city, this is the place to visit.

Guides and Services

The Amsterdam City Tourist Office (V.V.V.)

Main Office, off Dam Square at 5 Rokin   Tel: 66 66 6
Open 9:00 AM to 5:30 PM every day. A second office, in front of the rail station, is open till midnight. Considerable material on all cultural events is available at both places.

Living Guide to Amsterdam

Published in 1975 as part of the festivities associated with the city's Septcentennial (700 years!), this is the most helpful English-language guide to the youth-oriented city of Amsterdam. Available at major hotels and newsstands. Other guidebooks, including KLM's own *Surprising Amsterdam,* should also prove useful.

Opera Houses and Concert Halls

Theater Carré

111-125 Amstel   Tel: 22 61 77
Season: full year, including ballet, opera, concerts, plays, musical comedy, reviews. Performances usually start at 8:00 PM.
Box Office: open daily 10:00 AM to 8:00 PM.   Tel: 22 52 25
There are over a hundred authorized ticket agencies.
Seating Capacity: 1800.
Street clothes are perfectly acceptable when attending performances in this old horseshoe-shaped circus theater built by Oskar Carré. Although ticket prices do vary, the accent is on low cost. Matinees are less expensive. Visibility is excellent from all seats. We witnessed a delightful performance of Rameau's *Platée* here.

Stadsschouwburg (Municipal Theater)

Nickname: "Huis op het Plein" (House on the Square)

Leidseplein   Tel: 24 91 90

Season: all year, presenting ballet, opera, plays, operettas, cabaret. During July
    and first half of August, no opera or drama. Matinees usually start at 1:30
    PM and evening performances at 8:15 PM.

Box Office: open daily 10:00 AM to 6:30 PM.   Tel: 23 39 32
    Tickets may also be obtained at Tourist Information Offices. The main
    Tourist Office (V.V.V.) in front of the central station is open daily,
    including Sunday from 9:00 AM to midnight. Another, at Rokin 5, is open
    daily from 9:00 AM to 5:30 PM.   Tel: 66 44 4

Seating Capacity: 950.

Various national groups (Nederlandse Comedie, Toneelgroep Theatre, and the
National Ballet) use this theater, but aside from ballet, opera is the most
accessible entertainment for foreigners inasmuch as it is usually presented in its
original language, not in Dutch. The Netherlands Opera makes its home here.

Het Concertgebouw (The Concertgebouw Orchestra)

6 J. W. Brouwersplein   Tel: 79 98 71; 79 29 86

Public Entrance: 98 van Baerlestraat

Season: September to July including concerts and chamber recitals (large and
    small hall). Closed December 5, December 31, January 1, Good Friday,
    and Easter Sunday. Concerts start at 8:00 PM or 8:15 PM.

Box Office: open Monday to Friday 10:00 AM to 3:00 PM (also on Saturday and
    Sunday if concerts take place then).

Seating Capacity: 2207 in large hall.

Tickets are in great demand and should be reserved in advance. Everybody but
everybody—including hotel and motel personnel—knows what's on at the
Concertgebouw. Distances are often measured from the building, one of the
most acoustically perfect in the world. Now led by Bernard Haitink, the
orchestra was under the direction of the famous conductor, Willem Mengelberg,
for almost fifty years. After the war, Eduard van Beinum was its director. They
made the orchestra one of the great musical organizations of Western Europe.

From every seat in the auditorium you have a perfect view. Some of the
least expensive seats are *behind* the orchestra, where you have a full view of the
conductor's activities, but the players themselves are in front of you. This is the
home of the Concertgebouw Orchestra, but when they are not performing, the
hall is used by soloists and chamber groups as well. The small hall, too, is used
by ensembles, soloists, and jazz groups. Amsterdam today is a center for modern
jazz.

The Dutch traditionally love good music. Their government follows suit.
The state, the province of North-Holland, and the city of Amsterdam together
contribute about sixty percent of the total appropriation for the orchestra.

Famous composers, among them Richard Strauss, Gustav Mahler, Claude Debussy, Max Reger, Maurice Ravel, Arnold Schoenberg, Igor Stravinsky, and others have come to Amsterdam to conduct their own compositions with the Concertgebouw. Mengelberg not only introduced Mahler's work to the Dutch, but also began an annual Mahler Festival in 1920. Mengelberg, too, initiated the annual performance of Bach's *St. Matthew's Passion,* and the yearly Beethoven cycle. Pierre Monteux and Bruno Walter were two other well-known first conductors of the Concertgebouw, an orchestra of about 103 players.

Libraries and Museums

Toonkunst Bibliotheek and Openbare Muziekbibliotheek [Ben. 3]
59 Eerste Jacob van Campenstraat   Tel: 71 30 91
Hours: Monday to Friday, Saturday morning, and Tuesday and Friday evenings. No lending for home use on any morning or Wednesday afternoon. During July and August, open only Tuesday, Thursday, Saturday.
Both libraries serve the Institut voor Muziekwetenschap of the University of Amsterdam, located at the same address. Since 1960, the Toonkunst Bibliotheek has housed the library of the Vereniging voor Nederlandse Muziekgeschiedenis (The Association for Netherlands Musical History), which was formerly on deposit in the library of the University of Amsterdam.

Universiteitsbibliotheek [Ben. 4]
425 Singel   Tel: 21 78 78
Hours: Monday to Friday and Saturday morning; slightly restricted during July and August.

Toneelmuseum (Theater Museum)
168 Herengracht   Tel: 23 39 93
Hours for Museum: Monday to Saturday 10:00 AM to 5:00 PM; Sunday and holidays 1:00 PM to 5:00 PM.
Hours for Library: Monday to Friday 10:00 AM to 5:00 PM. Closed New Year's Day.
Transportation: Tramways No. 1, 2, 13, 17 from Central Station.
No credentials necessary.
The Dutch Wagner Vereniging (Society) has headquarters here.
    An exhibit entitled *Muziek in Amsterdam* was displayed at the Toneelmuseum from November 15, 1975 to January 18, 1976. The joint Toonkunst- and Openbare Muziekbibliotheek organized the material and published a 38-page catalogue of the display, which spans the period from Sweelinck's time to the present. A prominent place was given to the history of organs in Holland.

Theater Klank en Beeld

168 Herengracht   Tel: 65 74 2
Hours: Monday to Friday 9:00 AM to 5:00 PM; no annual closing.
No fee or credentials necessary.

Amsterdam City Archives (Gemeentelijke Archiefdienst)

67 Amsteldijk and also an auxiliary building at
55 Nieuwe Prinzengracht   Tel: 21 44 55; 76 31 31
Hours: winter weekdays 9:00 AM to 5:00 PM; Saturday 9:00 AM to noon; summer
  weekdays only, 9:00 AM to 5:00 PM. Closed New Year's Day, Easter
  Monday, Ascension Day, Whit Monday, Christmas, Queen's Birthday
  (April 30), and Liberation Day (5 May).
No credentials necessary; open to all who wish to use library for study purposes.
Archivists employed by the city often publish material pertaining to Amster-
dam. Recently, The Stichting (Foundation) H.J. Duyvis Funds has provided
the financial support for the publication of other studies relating to the city.

Stichting Donemus (Donemus Foundation)

51 Jacob Obrechtstraat (at corner of De Lairessestraat)   Tel: 72 24 32
Hours: Monday to Friday 9:00 AM to 5:00 PM. No annual holidays or closing.
Transportation: Trams 2, 3, 16, and Bus 26.
No admission fees or credentials.
Facilities include reproduction equipment and working space. Contents include
about 50,000 items. The main collection comprises some 4000 scores of
contemporary Dutch composers; much of this music on tape or records as well.
The collection also includes scores of Dutch composers of fifteenth to nineteenth
centuries, as well as twentieth-century scores by other nationals. Both scores and
parts may be loaned or purchased from this library. Donemus functions as
Holland's Music Information Center. Music published by Donemus is listed in
catalogs; music includes material for orchestra, chamber groups, vocal groups,
carillon music (issued with the Netherlands Carillon Society, see below), and
music for the young (with local branch of Jeunesses Musicales). Donemus also
publishes *Sonorum Speculum* (see below) a quarterly devoted to Dutch musical
life.

Institut voor Dialectologie, Volkskunde en Naamkunde

569–571 Keizersgracht   Tel: 23 46 98
Hours: Monday to Friday 9:30 AM to 5:15 PM. No annual holidays or closing.
Transportation: trams 16, 24, 25 from Central Station.
No admission fees or credentials.
Folklore department deals with Dutch folksong—printed, written, and re-
corded.

Nederlands Volkslied Archief (Netherlands Folksong Archive)
7 Nicolaas Maesstraat
This archive is intended to be a study center for those interested in obtaining scientific or practical information on any aspect of Dutch folksongs. To achieve this goal, old songs and melodies—either in print or passed down by oral tradition—are copied and classified into groups, while a library is also being formed. Over 25,000 songs have been cataloged. We are, however, missing more up-to-date information on this center.

Study Center for Music Libraries
59 Eerste Jacob van Campenstraat
All public music libraries, as well as public reading rooms with a music section, are affiliated with this central organization. The Study Center promotes the training of assistants for music libraries and cooperates in the production of a Central Catalog of Music (in preparation), a part of which is already housed in the Royal Library in The Hague. This Center cooperates in the preparation of RISM (Répertoire International des Sources Musicales). See the article on the Center in *Fontes* (1974), p. 96 ff.

Etnomusicologisch Centrum "Jaap Kunst" (formerly Library of the Ethnological Music Section of the Royal Institute for the Tropics)
103 Kloveniersburgwal   Tel: 23 34 16
Hours: by appointment from 9:00 AM to 5:00 PM daily.

"Musica in Numis" Collection
176 Kalverstraat
This collection of about 1300 commemorative medals, medallions, coins, and plaques with reproductions of composers, conductors, musicologists, and performers of all times is the private property of the publisher, Johan A. Alsbach. The medals date from as far back as the fifteenth century. The oldest piece shows the Dutch musicologist, Nicolaus Schliffer, and was struck in bronze in 1457, by Boldu. The collection also contains 95 different medallions of Beethoven, 80 of Mozart, and a few of Verdi, Schubert, Handel, Liszt, Haydn, Johann Strauss, Jr., Rossini, Brahms, Chopin, Gluck, and Mahler. A particularly beautiful Beethoven medallion was struck by the Dutch firm Koninklijke Begeer, and a medal by Galambos (1903, issued on the occasion of Hugo Wolf's death) also deserves mention. A coin of Rouget de Lisle contains the entire text of the "Marseillaise" on one side. The smallest coin holds a portrait of Schubert. The collection is seen by appointment only.

Koninklijke Instituut voor de Tropen (Royal Institute for the Tropics)
2a Linnaeusstraat
Main building is at 63 Mauritskade.

Instrument collection of the Library of the Ethnological Music Section.
Hours: March 1 to November 1, Monday to Saturday 10:00 AM to 5:00 PM; Sunday and holidays noon to 5:00 PM. November 1 to March 1, Monday to Saturday 10:00 AM to 4:00 PM; Sunday and holidays noon to 4:00 PM.
This collection contains about 1880 instruments—270 chordophones, 530 idiophones, 380 membranophones, and 700 aerophones in the Sachs/von Hornbostel terminology—consisting mainly of instruments from the Indonesian archipelago, including three complete gamelan orchestras from Java and Bali. There are also instruments from New Guinea, Africa, and other tropical regions.

Ets Haim Library of Sephardic Community Center

Mailing Address: c/o Portuguese Synagogue, 197 Rapenburgerstraat
Entrance: 3 Visserplein   Tel: 24 53 51
Hours: Sunday 9:00 AM to 1:00 PM.
The Jewish community has always been well treated by the Dutch, many of whom risked their lives offering them protection during the Nazi Occupation. Particularly in Amsterdam, which had a large Jewish population before the War, Hebrew and Yiddish expressions became part of the vernacular. For example, the Septcentennial celebration in Amsterdam in 1975 was called "Mokum 700." And Mokum is the Hebrew noun for "place." Amsterdamers refer to their town as the Mokum, the Place. The Ets Haim Library and the main Synagogue on Rembrandtsplein managed to stay intact during the Occupation because they were considered landmarks belonging to a friendly nation (Spain).

Conservatories and Schools

Amsterdam Conservatorium
5-7 Bachstraat

Universiteit van Amsterdam, Instituut voor Muziekwetenschap (Institute of Musicology)
59 Eerste Jacob van Campenstraat
The faculty in the past had consisted of Professor Dr. Jos. Smits van Waesberghe (Middle Ages), and Jaap Kunst (Ethnomusicology). Professor Frank Harrison is head of the ethnomusicology unit now (see *Libraries*).

Institute for Medieval Musicology
19 Staalstraat
This institute, founded by its current director, has been placed at the disposal of

the Municipal University of Amsterdam. Begun in 1934, it now has more than 30,000 photocopies of medieval music, taken from the originals held in libraries, museums, and collections throughout the world.

Musical Organizations

Foundation Donemus, Documentatie in Nederland voor Muziek (Documentation in the Netherlands for Music)

51 Jacob Obrechtstraat   Tel: 72 24 32

The Foundation "Netherlands Musical Interests" was responsible in May 1947 for the establishment of the Foundation Donemus to promote knowledge of contemporary Dutch music. Donemus makes available, to performing musicians, the works of contemporary Dutch composers for which no commercial editions seemed justified or possible. Of course, particularly in a small country with a limited home market, this means virtually most compositions by modern masters. In this respect, Donemus consequently takes the place of the normal publisher. Using photographic duplicating processes, Donemus itself makes copies of manuscript scores and of parts written out by professional copyists. According to international custom, chamber music is sold on performance, and orchestral works are hired out. The composer's royalty is fifteen percent of the selling price and two-thirds of the hiring fee.

A section for documentation contains all information such as biographies, guides and analyses of works, criticisms and press clippings from the international press, reference works and articles that refer in any way to contemporary Dutch music. (For Donemus's library, see above.) In its auditorium, works may be heard on records or tape between 9:00 AM and 5:00 PM Monday through Friday.

Donemus publishes a quarterly journal, *Sonorum Speculum* (Mirror of Musical Life), in English and German. It contains articles on Dutch composers and their works as well as information about Dutch musical life. It is distributed free of charge (see *Periodicals*).

Donemus publishes a vocal and instrumental catalog that includes both the works "published" by Donemus and those editions of Dutch works handled by commercial publishers. The Foundation prepares and distributes the Donemus Audio Visual Series (DAV Series) of Dutch music on records with scores. Four records appear annually.

As far as orchestral works are concerned, they are recorded live and are intended for those who place greater store on becoming acquainted with a work than on technical perfection of the recording and performance. With this series, the Foundation intends to stress the documentary value of Dutch composers and their works. Donemus also publishes a catalog of the recording series.

Working with Radio Nederland, every season Donemus presents in its auditorium a series of chamber music concerts devoted to contemporary Dutch and foreign composers. Records of these concerts, made by Radio Nederland, are offered for transmission by foreign radio stations.

Donemus receives significant subsidies from the government, the city of Amsterdam, the province of North Holland, and the Foundation "Netherlands Musical Interests."

Amsterdam Kunstraad (Amsterdam Arts Council)
Town Hall, Room 20a, O.Z. 199 Voorburgwal

Stichting Muziek Centrum (Foundation Music Center)
458 Herengracht
This organization owns the building that houses the Concertgebouw Orchestra offices, Donemus, Jeugd en Muziek, and other organizations. It aids musical groups by making various premises available to them.

Het Nederlands Instituut voor Internationael Cultureel Betrekkingen (The Netherlands Institute for International Cultural Relations)
41 J.J. Viottastraat
The Institute strengthens cultural bonds between Holland and foreign countries. It also gives financial support for publication of *Sonorum Speculum* and it organizes foreign tours for Dutch performers.

Nederlands Bartók Genootschap (Netherlands Bartók Society)
50 Joh. Meeuwisstraat
In order to promote knowledge of Bartók's compositions, the society publishes Bartók's letters and writings in Dutch, and maintains both a library of his works and a record collection of his compositions.

Opera Piccola Amsterdam
405 Hoofweg
This group brings simple, intimate performances of opera to everyone, especially those with low incomes. They tour Holland with "Shadow Performances" (as they call them) of important fragments of Mozart's operas played in costume and interrupted by short explanations. Arias and ensembles are in the original language, the rest is in Dutch.

Jeugd en Muziek (Youth and Music)
Central Office, 51 Jacob Obrechtstraat
There are branches at Alkmaar, Amersfoot, Amsterdam, Doorn, Eindhoven, Groningen, The Hague, Hilversum, Hoogeveen, Kennemerland, Krimpenerwaard, Leeuwarden, Maarssen, Naarden, Nieuwer-Amstel, Roermond, Rotter-

dam, Utrecht, Zaandam, Zeist, and Zwolle, as well as twenty-five other local groups that are affiliated with Youth and Music and benefit from their facilities.

The Society aims at bringing Dutch youth from the ages of 11 to 25 into closer contact with music by seeing that music is made for, by, and with young people. For young people, they organize concerts sometimes with annotated programs; provide film programs about music; give musical information and training; arrange meetings and lectures locally, regionally, nationally, and internationally on an exchange basis, and see that its members obtain a reduction in ticket prices for concerts, recitals, ballet and opera performances, etc., organized by other new institutions.

To stimulate musicmaking by young people, they have youth orchestras and choirs under the direction of professionals. In their repertoire, arrangements are avoided and they play only original works, particularly those by Dutch composers. In association with Donemus (see above), Youth and Music publishes a catalog of orchestral and chamber works by contemporary Dutch composers written and/or particularly intended for young performers. School groups can then obtain this material at lower rates.

The Society was begun originally by Sem Dresden as a foundation and changed into a society in 1956, when it became affiliated with the International Jeunesses Musicales, with headquarters in Brussels. It now has over 6000 members, and the organization fosters record clubs, folk dancing, and other group activities in addition to the ones mentioned above.

Nederlands Theater Centrum (Netherlands Theater Center)
186 Singel

This organization makes it possible for employees from all types of industries to be placed in a position to attend the best plays, operas, concerts, films, and ballets at reduced prices. Ticket fees are payable in ten monthly installments.

Miscellaneous

The Hollandsche Schouwburg
Plantage Middenlaan

In the center of Amsterdam stands a monument, the Hollandsche Schouwburg. No longer a theater, it is today a memorial to the suffering of the Jewish community of Amsterdam during the Second World War. In September 1941, the Jewish inhabitants of the Netherlands were forbidden by the Nazi authorities to take part in any form of artistic expression. They were unable to perform in theaters, concert halls, and films. The Hollandsche Schouwburg then came into use as a specifically Jewish theater where discharged Jewish artists performed for an exclusively Jewish audience. One year later the building was converted to another function.

In July 1942, the *Endlösung der Judenfrage*, the final solution to the Jewish question, commenced throughout Europe, and the Germans began to deport Jews from all Nazi-occupied countries to the gas chambers of Poland. The Schouwburg was outfitted as the local concentration center and transit depot. The theater of the Jews thus became their prison. Families dragged from their homes were detained here until enough were collected for transportation to their first stop, the Westerbork concentration camp. Sanitary conditions were deplorable. The inhuman treatment of the prisoners accorded with the National Socialist patterns of behavior. Although no accurate figures can be given for the number of Jews who found the Hollandsche Schouwburg their last place of residence in Amsterdam, it has been estimated at 50,000.

In 1950, the former Hollandsche Schouwburg was presented to the city of Amsterdam by the Foundation Hollandsche Schouwburg, on condition that whatever the future use of the building might be, it must contain a memorial, an eternal light to serve as a continuing reminder of the fate of the Amsterdam Jews. By this time, the building was in terrible need of repair. Part of it was torn down, other parts renovated. The walls of the former stage were left intact, and the ceiling was removed. Today there is a plateau between the walls, and an obelisk of basaltic lava rises from a supporting base shaped in the form of a Star of David. On the walls enclosing this grassy courtyard is an inscription in Dutch and in Hebrew: "In memory of those who were taken away from this place 1940–1945." The earth and the subtropical plants here come from Israel. A more introspective chapel with an eternal light is in a front hall linking the courtyard and the outside. The upper floors of the Schouwburg are used for cultural purposes.

A visit here is an unforgettable experience.

The Business of Music

Except for New York and Tel Aviv, Amsterdam has more book stores than any other city. Many of these carry books about music. One of the foremost Antiquarian shops is that managed by Saul B. Groen at 6 Ferdinand Bolstraat. His telephone number is 76 22 40.

Publishers
Alsbach & Co.
11 Leidsegracht   Tel: 22 26 26
Annie Bank
13 Anna Vondelstraat   Tel: 85 48 3

Broeckmans & Van Poppel
92 van Baerlestraat   Tel: 72 80 84
C.B. Smit
52 Amstel   Tel: 23 88 00
Donemus
51 Jacob Obrechtstraat (see *Musical Organzations; Libraries*)   Tel: 72 24 32
Editions Altona
90 Vondelstraat   Tel: 18 63 24
Edition Heuwekemeijer
1 Bredeweg   Tel: 53 08 6
Edition J. Nagel
35 Weteringschans   Tel: 64 66 4
Firma J. Poeltuyn
18 Deurlostraat   Tel: 72 28 27
Holland Music
500 Singel   Tel: 23 11 63
Les Éditions Int. Basart N.V.
11 Leidsegracht (see also *Alsbach*)   Tel: 22 26 26
Metro Muziek
18 B. Zweerskade   Tel: 72 31 16
Muziekuitgeverij Melodia (see *C. Smit,* publishers)
New Sound
75 Rooseveltlaan   Tel: 71 20 21
Panda Productions
41 Nic. Maesstraat
Universal Songs N.V.
52 Vossiusstraat

HOLLAND, GENERAL

Opera Houses and Concert Halls

The Hague   *Tel. prefix: (070)*

Koninklijke Schouwburg (Royal Theater)
3 Korte Voorhout   Tel: 11 62 70
Season: all year except July and August, presenting plays, opera, ballet.
Box Office: open 9:00 AM to 3:00 PM daily   Tel: 18 44 50
Seating Capacity: 781.

Circustheater, Scheveningen
50 Gevers Deynootplein (public entrance)   Tel: 54 69 00
Season: all year, offering opera, ballet, recitals, musicals, concerts, one-man
   shows.
Box Office: 2e Messstraat (that *is* the correct spelling for the mailing address).
Hours: 10:00 AM to 4:00 PM daily; tickets go on sale about three days before a
   given performance.
Seating Capacity: 1500-1600 seats, depending on type of performance.
There are about thirty authorized ticket agencies for this theater. Evening dress
is usually worn for operas or ballet galas, but street dress is acceptable for most
performances.

Rotterdam   *Tel. prefix: (010)*

Concert and Congresscentre "de Doelen"
50 Schouwburgplein   Tel: 14 29 11
Season: all year, with highlights from October through July, presenting classical
   concerts (symphonic and chamber), and pop, and jazz.
Box Office: 2 Kruisstraat (near public entrance to hall)   Tel: 13 24 90
Hours: daily from 10:00 AM to 4:00 PM; in addition, a phone call to 13 13 70
   during these hours will provide you with program information; on Sunday,
   the box office is open from noon to 4:00 PM.
Seating Capacity: large hall, 2200; small hall, 600; ten other halls accommodating
   30 to 350.
This very modern building, opened May 18, 1966, is the largest auditorium in
Europe. Its acoustical properties are magnificent. The building contains a
restaurant, conference rooms, and a permanent art gallery. Many business
executives hold regular meetings here. The hall also has superb arrangements
for simultaneous translations, thereby making it an excellent location for
international meetings. Opening twenty-six years to the month after the total
destruction of the city of Rotterdam, "de Doelen" stands as a monument to the
Dutch determination to rebuild their land after the war.

Libraries and Museums

The 1977 *Directory of Music and Record Libraries in the Netherlands* (Gids van
muziekbibliotheken en fonotheken in Nederland), 2nd. ed., has been published
by Nederlands Bibliotheek en Lektuurcentrum. Available by mail from P.O.
Box 2054, The Hague, it contains detailed information on fifty-seven public,
special, and research music libraries and forty-two record libraries.

Berg en Dal

Africa Museum
Meerwijk, Berg en Dal
Hours: Monday to Saturday, 9:00 AM to 12:30 PM; 1:30 PM to 5:00 PM and by
    appointment; Sundays and holidays, 10:00 AM to 12:30 PM, 1:30 PM to 5:00
    PM.
This museum contains a collection of close to a hundred different African wind
and percussion instruments, mainly from Angola, the Belgian Congo, West and
East Africa.

Bussum

Van Leeuwen Boomkamp Collection
(Plucked and stringed instruments)
19 Willemslaan
This collection consists of close to forty instruments, including old Italian
seventeenth- and eighteenth-century plucked instruments, dancing masters'
violins (kits), gambas, lutes, a Clementi Hammerklavier dating from 1810, a
collection of bows, and an archive of prints and reproductions relating to these
instruments.

Enschede

Frederika Menko Warendorf Stichting (Foundation)

125 Klanderij, Enschede
Hours: Monday, 3:00 PM to 6:00 PM; 7:00 PM to 9:00 PM; Tuesday to Friday, 10:00
    AM to 1:00 PM, 3:00 PM to 6:00 PM, 7:00 PM to 9:00 PM; Saturday, 10:00 AM to
    1:00 PM. No annual closing.
No admission fee; borrowers must be members of Public Library.
Facilities: some reproduction equipment available.

The Hague (Den Haag or 's Gravenhage)

Koninklijk Conservatorium voor Muziek, Bibliotheek
7 Korte Beestenmarkt   Tel: 63 99 25

Openbare Muziekbibliotheek (Public Library)
1 Bilderdijkstraat   Tel: 33 38 46
Hours: Tuesday to Friday, 10:00 AM to 5:30 PM; Monday, noon to 5:30 PM;
    Saturday, 10:00 AM to 1:00 PM; Monday, Wednesday, Friday evenings, 7:00
    PM to 9:00 PM. No annual closings.

Koninklijke Bibliotheek [Ben. 9]

34 Lange Voorhout   Tel: 18 46 26

Hours: Monday to Friday and Saturday morning. Closed two weeks in mid-
summer.

Koninklijk Huisarchief (Royal Archives) [Ben. 10]

74 Noordeinde   Tel: 60 07 56

Hours: Monday to Friday. Closed Christmas, New Year's, Good Friday, Easter,
Pentecost, April 30, June 29.

For access, write Director in advance.

Haags Gemeentemuseum (Municipal Museum), Muziekafdeling
(Music Section) [Ben. 8]

41 Stadhouderslaan   Tel: 51 41 81

Hours: Monday to Saturday 10:00 AM to 5:00 PM; Sunday 1:00 PM to 5:00 PM;
Wednesday 8:00 PM to 10:00 PM.

Free admission to the library; small fee for the instrument collection. The music
department of the Municipal Museum consists of two parts: a large collection of
musical instruments and a music research library. Both are located in the city's
new Museum of Modern Art. The library originated in 1935 with the purchase
of the Scheurleer collection of musical instruments and books on music.
Recently, catalogs have been published under the guidance of Dr. van Gleich.
The museum building itself is the last important commission of the architect,
H.P. Berlage.

The instrument collection is one of the finest in Europe. The displays are
carefully labeled and cassette guides are available to visitors enabling them to
hear the various instruments they are viewing. We must remember that the
Netherlands had been actively engaged in commerce and industry with the East
Indian islands, and for this reason numerous examples of Eastern instruments
can be seen throughout Holland. The staff of this collection, under the guidance
of Dr. van Gleich, has truly led the way for all future displays of instruments.

Leiden

Rijksmuseum voor Volkenkunde (National Museum of Ethnology)

la Steenstraat

Hours: From February 17 through October, Monday to Friday 10:00 AM to 5:00
PM; from November 1 to February 16, Monday to Friday 10:00 AM to 4:00
PM; Sunday and holidays open from 1:00 PM to 5:00 PM. Closed January 1
and October 3. A special study collection may be visited only by special
arrangement.

This collection of about two hundred instruments is not displayed in one place. Instead, the instruments are distributed among the sections devoted to various countries, in particular Japan, India, Indonesia, (see the gamelan orchestra), Africa, and New Guinea.

Rijksuniversiteit, Bibliotheek [Ben. 19]
70–74 Rapenburg (mail address: P.O. Box 58)
Hours: Monday to Saturday.

Nieuw-Loosdrecht

Will Jansen Collection (Bassoons)
4 Eikenlaan, Nieuw-Loosdrecht, near Haarlem
Begun as a hobby in the spring of 1949, the collection now contains twenty-three bassoons. The oldest instrument dates from 1740, while the rarest instrument is a Karl Almenraeder bassoon dating from 1821 and made by the Mainz bassoonmaker, August Jehring. Only three examples of this instrument, the forerunner of the modern bassoon, are known. Also available here is an archive consisting of photos, drawings, etc., of the instrument, and biographies of 590 bassoonmakers from all parts of the world, the earliest of which is dated 1548.

Rotterdam

Gemeente-Bibliotheek [Ben. 20]
1 Nieuwe markt   Tel: 13 50 40
Hours: different hours from Monday to Saturday.

Museum of Geography and Ethnology
25 Willemskade
Hours: daily from 10:00 AM to 5:00 PM. Closed January 1.
The Museum contains about 120 musical instruments from Africa, North and South America, Indonesia, and Oceania.

Utrecht

Bibliotheek Instituut voor Muziekwetenschap der Rijksuniversiteit
[Ben. 21]
21 Drift   Tel: (030) 1 68 41

Hours: Monday to Friday, 9:00 AM to 5:00 PM. Closed Easter, Christmas, "Pinksteren" (Whitsunday).
In answering our questionnaire, the staff calls their organization "one of the largest musicological libraries in Europe."

National Museum "Van Speeldoos tot Pierement"
(National Museum "From Music Box to Barrel Organ")
38 Lange Nieuwestraat
Hours: Thursday and Friday evening, 7:30 PM to 10:00 PM; Saturday and Sunday 2:00 PM to 5:00 PM. For viewing at other times, apply to Curator, Jul. Jongenelen, 24 Copijnlaan, Utrecht.
This museum owns a collection of automatic musical instruments including old clocks, music boxes, old organs, and instruments illustrating the development of the Dutch barrel organ or *pierement.*

Conservatories and Schools

Higher education in Holland is provided by universities and other institutions of university level which specialize in certain fields of study like economics, agriculture, music, medicine, technology, and art. The academic year extends from the middle of September to July and is not divided into semesters. The Netherlands Office for Foreign Student Relations publishes *A Student Travel Guide to the Netherlands,* available through U.S. Office, Pier 40, North River, New York, N.Y. 10014; *Vadecum,* a concise guide for foreign students in the Netherlands, is published by the Foreign Student Service; *Higher Education and Research in the Netherlands* (The Hague) is a quarterly published by the Netherlands Universities Foundation for International Cooperation (NUFFIC). The last two publications may be obtained through the auspices of The Netherlands Information Service, 711 Third Avenue, New York, N.Y. 10020.

All the following schools have courses in instrumental music, voice, conducting, composition, and music theory. In addition, The Hague Royal Music Conservatory has courses in dance.

Amersfoort

Stichting Nederlandse Beiaardschool (Dutch Carillon School)
7 Muurhuizen

The Hague

Koninklijk Conservatorium voor Muziek (Royal Conservatory of Music)
7 Korte Beestenmarkt   Tel: 63 99 25
Note for foreign students: the scholastic year starts January 1, but foreign students may be enrolled at any time. Some scholarships are granted by the Dutch government to foreign students if their countries have an agreement in this field with the Netherlands. Further information can be obtained from the Dutch Embassy in the country.

Leiden

Muziekgeschiedenis der Rijksuniversiteit
106 Rapenburg   Tel: (017) 102 20 44

Rotterdam

Rotterdams Toonkunst Conservatorium (Rotterdam Music Conservatory)
219 Mathenesser Laan

Utrecht

Nederlands Instituut voor Katholieke Kerkmuziek
(Dutch Institute for Catholic Church Music)
5 Plompetorengracht

School voor Protestants Kerkmuziek (School for Protestant Church Music)
2 Lange Nieuwstraat

Utrechts Conservatorium
2–4 Lange Nieuwstraat

Rijksuniversiteit Utrecht (State University of Utrecht)
Instituut voor Muziekwetenschap (Institute of Musicology)
21 Drift (Institute at la Rijknkade)   Tel: (030) 1 68 41
Musicology as a discipline in Holland began here in 1929 at the State University of Utrecht. In 1930 the Institute was founded. Professor Dr. Smijers was the first Professor of Musicology.

Rijksuniversiteit Utrecht, Studio voor Electronische Muziek
(State University of Utrecht, Studio for Electronic Music)
14–16 Plompetorengracht
Write for catalog from Bureau Curatoren der Rijksuniversiteit.

Summer Schools

Haarlem

Summer Academy for Organists
Stadhuis
Prerequisites: for working students, Staatsdiploma B or a final diploma for the organ from a Dutch or foreign conservatory.

For the first three weeks in July, the Academy gives courses to young organists under the approved direction of internationally known artists and experts. Improvisation and interpretation are treated from various points of view. The courses are given on the Müller organ in the Great (St. Bavo) Church and on the Cavaille-Coll organ in the Haarlem Concertgebouw.

The sessions begin at the same time as the annual organ contest held here in July. Among past teachers, Henk Badings is most important.

's-Hertogenbosch

's-Hertogenbosch Summer Course for Vocalists
Stichting 's-Hertogenbosch Muziekstad, Town Hall, 's-Hertogenbosch
Opera, lied, and oratorio study for professional and pre-professional singers under 40 years of age.

Hilversum

Conductors' Course of the Netherlands Radio Union
Post Box 150
Prerequisite: working students must not be older than 36. At a competitive entrance exam, the candidates must also give proof of their ability to conduct an orchestra.

An international course for conductors is offered here for five weeks in June and July, generally under the guidance of two world-famous conductors. Dutch and foreign working members and auditors are admitted in limited numbers.

Queekhoven, Breukelen

An International Lute Week
Eduard van Beinum Stichting
Dates: about the first week in June.
Courses: performance practice and music for Renaissance lute, Baroque lute, theorbo, and chitarrone; also the construction of the lute in relation to historical instruments of the lute family; a comparison with the same developments for harpsichord and other stringed instruments.
Lectures and concerts are also offered here.

Musical Organizations

Bilthoven

Stichting Gaudeamus
(Foundation "Gaudeamus")
21 Gerard Doulaan   Tel: (030) 78 70 33
Gaudeamus aims to make contacts among musicians, support them, and further
their knowledge of music. There are three sections: a concert platform within
which concerts are organized; a music atheneum that organizes lectures and
discussion evenings, maintains a library of contemporary works, and cooperates
in the publication of music; a composers section that fosters relationships
among older and younger composers. Huize Gaudeamus once belonged to the
composer, Julius Rontgen (1855–1932). A young composer staying there today
has the opportunity to work without distractions; and because other composers
are also in residence, he is prevented from suffering musical isolation, by being
exposed at the same time to their works.

Haarlem

Foundation "Nieuwe Muziek"
9 Spaarnelaan

The Hague

Vereniging voor Nederlandse Muziekgeschiedenis (Society for Netherlands Musical History)
23 Fagotstraat, Rijswijk, Z.H.   Tel: 98 24 96
Founded in 1868, this group aims to make a scientific study of Dutch music and
its history. It organizes study meetings, makes microfilms of works by Dutch
composers, and provides copies of these for study purposes. Certain works are
available in full score. A series of radio programs is presented, concerts are
promoted, and exhibitions are organized. The works of Obrecht, Josquin Des
Prez, Sweelinck, and others have been published under its auspices. This society
is a member of the Société Internationale de Musicologie (International
Musicological Society).

Nederlands Cultureel Contact (Netherlands Cultural Contact)
4 Nachtegaalplein
This is a consultation center for all matters regarding Dutch cultural life.

Alg. Ndl. Unie van Muziekverenigingen (General Dutch Union for Music Associations)
1496 Hoefkade

Raad voor de Kunst (Arts Council)
66 Zeestraat
They advise the Minister of Education, Arts, and Science regarding the government's obligation in the field of music, music-drama, dance, literature, cinema, folk art, and the aesthetic training of the young.

Stichting Voor Oude Nederlands Muziek (Foundation for Old Netherlands Music)
13 Dr. A. Kuyperstraat
This group promotes the study of Dutch vocal and instrumental music of the seventeenth and eighteenth centuries. It publishes a series of practical editions of early Dutch music.

Hilversum

Nederlandtsche Gedenck-Clanck
24 Van der Helstlaan
This group, whose name defies easy translation—except that it means commemorative sonority—tries to make authentic musical material available from Dutch history for the purpose and promotion of national celebrations and festivals both in Holland and abroad.

Stichting Jacob Obrecht (Jacob Obrecht Foundation)
24 Van der Helstlaan
This organization devotes itself primarily to promoting the music of Obrecht at home and abroad. It encourages the Netherlands Chamber Choir, the Motet Choir of the Netherlands Bach Society, etc. to perform music by Obrecht (see introductory essay).

(Nederlandse Guitaristen Vereniging "Constantijn Huygens") "Constantijn Huygens" Netherlands Society for Guitarists
10 Hendrik de Keyserlaan
The 450 members of this group are dedicated to improving their guitar playing. They also want guitarists to receive a classical education so as to continue the tradition of erudite guitarists.

Stichting d'Oprechte Amateur (The "Dedicated" Amateur Foundation)
Post Box 209
The group promotes amateur musicmaking in all its forms.

Rotterdam

Vereniging van Muziekhandelaren en Uitgevers in Nederland (Society of Music Dealers and Publishers in the Netherlands)
132 Nieuwe Binnenweg

Nederlandse Organisten Vereniging (Society of Netherlands Organists)
39b Soetendaalseweg
They publish a monthly periodical called *Het Orgel* (The Organ).

Vereniging voor Huismuziek (Society for Domestic Music)
38a Berkelselaan
Unlike the French or Italians or even the Germans, the Dutch have no tradition of princely residences with their court orchestras which promoted the development of music in earlier times. For this reason, it has been customary in Holland for the people themselves to make music in their own homes, "Huismuziek," as they call it. Understandably then, this society seeks to preserve this very important facet of Dutch musical life. It publishes a journal, *Huismuziek*, that appears six times a year. The Society also has a subsidiary group, the Blokfluitcommissie, that influences the study of recorder playing in Holland.

Schagen

Mozart Vereniging (The Mozart Society)
Villa Ananda

Utrecht

Eduard van Beinum Stichting (Eduard van Beinum Foundation, sometimes called the International Musicians Center)
Huize "Queekhoven," 31 Zandpad, Breukelen
Not a music school or a conservatory, this "haven of art," where young musicians who have completed their studies can come for further work, discussions, and meetings with other musicians, has more than served its purpose. Over six hundred musicians from twenty different countries have found hospitality in this international center since its organization in 1960.

Fees depend on length of stay. Full board is offered visitors. Write to above address for brochure with complete information.

Stichting Moderne Muziek (Modern Music Foundation)
6 Gabriellaan
This group aims to promote contemporary music in all its forms, by organizing

lectures, record recitals, and discussion evenings, and providing annotations for modern works that are performed by the Utrecht Municipal Orchestra.

Nederlandse Dirigenten Organisation (Netherlands Conductors' Organization)
113a bis Biltstraat
This group includes 240 orchestral and choral conductors.

Instituut voor Muziekwetenschap (Institute of Musicology)
Mailing Address: c/o University of Utrecht, 21 Drift
Entrance: la Rijnkade   Tel: (030) 31 68 41
The Institute is part of the Rijksuniversiteit te Utrecht, Faculteit der Letteren. The current chairman is Dr. F.W.N. Hugenholtz, whose address is 29 Domplein, Utrecht; telephone number is (030) 25 35 1.

International Association of Sound Archives (IASA)
29 Hengeveldstraat
Membership in this recently established organization costs $3.00 a year for individuals and $10.00 a year for institutions.

There are, in general, four categories of archives or collections: national archives, broadcasting collections, public libraries, and privately operated collections. Some of the greatest sound archives in Europe are to be found in the broadcasting houses, but of course public access to these collections is not normally feasible. Dr. Schuursma currently edits the IASA journal, *The Phonographic Bulletin.* We must note that the Archives here in Utrecht include historical, literary, and dramatic material as well as musical items.

Wassenaar

De Pauwhof (The Peacock's Garden)
420 Rijksstraatweg
This country house, "De Pauwhof," allows artists and intellectuals a place to stay for a minimum of two weeks and as long as six months.

International Gustav Mahler Society
35 Narcislaan
The Dutch were among the first to recognize and support Mahler and his music. This society promotes performances, produces critical editions of his works, and has assembled a library and a collection of photos and recordings of Mahleriana.

The Business of Music

PUBLISHERS AND DEALERS

Amersfoort

Folia, Antiquarian Music
  Postbus 346

Bilthoven

Creyghton Musicology, Musica Antiqua
  45 Lassuslaan   Tel: (030) 78 37 14

Haarlem

Algemene Muziekhandel, W. Alphenaar
  49 Kruisweg   Tel: (023) 1 15 32

N.V. Grafische Industrie "De Toorts"
  1 Nijverheidsweg   Tel: (023) 1 52 38

The Hague ('s Gravenhage)

Muziekhandel Albersen en Co.
  182 Gr. Hertoginnelaan   Tel: (070) 33 73 33

Uitgeveril van Domburg
  32 Jan. Maetsuykerstraat   Tel: (070) 85 58 28

Krips Music
  71 Thorbeckelaan   Tel: (070) 68 96 55

Leo Smeets
  116 Roelofsstraat   Tel: (070) 24 85 56

Hilversum

Harmonia Uitgave
  23 Roeltjesweg   Tel: (021) 51 43 18

Uitgeverij J.J. Lispet
  Postbus 321   Tel: (021) 51 50 79

Rotterdam

Handelmij. Joh. de Heer & Zn.
  54 Jensiusstraat   Tel: (010) 24 18 71

W.F. Lichtenauer
     26 Korte Lijnbaan

Utrecht

J.R. Buschmann
     13 Lange Jansstraat   Tel: (030) 1 52 72

J.A. Wagenaar
     107–109 Oude Gracht   Tel: (030) 1 07 77

CONCERT MANAGERS

Bussum

Concertdirectie dr. G. de Koos
     43 Brediusweg

The Hague

Concertdirectie Johan Koning
     32 Ruychrocklaan

Nederlandse Concertdirectie J. Beek
     82 Koninginnegracht

Festivals

Amsterdam

Holland Festival
10 Honthorstraat   Tel: 72 33 20; 72 22 45
Dates: yearly, about June 15 to July 9, including ballet, opera, concerts, plays,
     film festival, special events (see *International Organ Contest* at Haarlem).
Box Office: 14 Haarlemstraat, Scheveningen (for mail subscriptions)
                                          Tel: 55 87 00
Hours: Sunday to Friday 10:00 AM to 4:00 PM.
Authorized ticket agencies are all over the Netherlands, particularly in Amsterdam, The Hague, and Rotterdam, and also in the United States at the Netherlands National Tourist Office in New York and the Mayfair Travel Service, Inc., 119 West 57 Street, New York, N.Y. 10019.

The Holland Festival is supported by the Dutch government as well as the cities of Amsterdam, Rotterdam, and The Hague. In Amsterdam, the Festival takes place mainly in the Stadsschouwburg (Municipal Theater) and the

Concertgebouw (Concert Hall); in The Hague, in the Koninklijke Schouwburg (Royal Theater) and the Netherlands Congress Building; in nearby Scheveningen on the North Sea coast, in the Circus Theater; in Rotterdam, in de Doelen (Concert Hall), and the Rotterdam Schouwburg (Municipal Theater). Participating groups include The Netherlands Opera, the Amsterdam Philharmonic, the Concertgebouw Orchestra, The Hague Residentie Orchestra, the Netherlands Chamber Orchestra, and the Rotterdam Philharmonic as well as orchestras and soloists from abroad. The latter have included the Deutsche Oper am Rhein from Düsseldorf, the London Sinfonietta, and the Royal Dramatic Theater of Stockholm. Chamber music concerts, choral concerts, ballet, and drama as well as early music concerts are all offered during the Holland Festival.

Apeldoorn

Opera Festival
V.V.V. Apeldoorn, 6 Stationsplein   Tel: (057) 60 12 49
Dates: annually from mid-July to mid-August.

Bilthoven

International Gaudeamus Music Week
Foundation Gaudeamus: Contemporary Music Center
P.O. Box 30   Tel: (030) 78 26 60
Dates: approximately the second week in September.
The Gaudeamus competitions for contemporary music are closely associated with this festival. A number of works are premiered in concerts in Amsterdam, Rotterdam, The Hague, Hilversum, and Utrecht. In addition, an analysis course is held daily in Bilthoven, and workshops for composers and interpreters are also offered.

Scheveningen

European International Song Festival
Mailing Address: V.V.V. Den Haag/Scheveningen, Gevers Deynootplein, Den Haag, Scheveningen.
Dates: July.
The headquarters of this festival are in Scheveningen, but the Festival itself is held every year in the country whose contestant won the competition the year before. It is often held at spas, such as Knokke in Belgium.

Competitions

Bilthoven

Gaudeamus International Competition for Interpreters of Contemporary Music
Foundation Gaudeamus, Contemporary Music Center
Post Box 30
Dates: about the first week in April.
Awards: first prize of 3000 fl.; four additional prizes.
Deadline: January; maximum age is 35; ensembles are limited to nine players; average age must not exceed 35 years.
The place of the competition generally varies.

Gaudeamus International Competition for Musical Composition
Foundation Gaudeamus, Contemporary Music Center
Post Box 30
Dates: about the second week in September.
Awards: cash prizes total 6,000 fl.
Deadline: January; maximum age is 35.
Entries for composers' competition must be sent in under a pseudonym. Both of these Bilthoven competitions are associated with the International Gaudeamus Music Week (see *Festivals*).

Haarlem

International Organ Improvisation Contest
Stadhuis
The contest usually takes place the first week in July. Five young organists of international reputation are invited to participate. Each contestant is placed in a separate room with a piano. One hour before their public appearance, the contestants are given a theme prepared each year by a different well-known musician. They are of course judged on their ability to improvise this theme, unknown to them until one hour before the performance. Organ concerts are also given during the competition.

The Hague

International Choir Festival
Write To: Emhage Tours, Inc., Att.: Concert Tours Division, 528 Keeler

Building, Grand Rapids, Michigan 45902
Dates: biennial event held in early June (odd-numbered years).
This competition is open to amateur choirs from all over the world. It is sponsored by the Federation of Dutch Singers Associations.

The address in Holland is: International Choir Festival, P.O. Box 496, The Hague, Holland.

's-Hertogenbosch

's-Hertogenbosch Competition for Singers
Concours International de Vocalistes
Stadhuis
Dates: usually September.
Awards: for each category of voice, one first prize of 2500 fl. and one second prize of 1000 fl. In addition, the best of the first prize winners is also awarded a concert in the Kleine Zaal of the Concertgebouw in Amsterdam.
Deadline: August 1. Contest is open to singers of both sexes and all nationalities up to the age of 34.
This competition includes lieder, oratorio, and opera.

Hilversum

International Carillon Contest
Stadhuis
Usually takes place in June.

Kerkrade

Foundation World Music Contest Kerkrade
13 Hoofdstraat
Dates: August, every four years, and lasts for a month.
Founded in 1950, this competition is devoted principally to wind and brass bands. Competition is open only to amateur groups: symphony orchestras, wind and brass bands, mandolin, and accordion groups.

Zwolle

Schnitgerprijs Zwolle International Composition Contest for Organ
Secretariaat, Stichting "Schnitgerprijs Zwolle," 2 Emmawijk
Awards: 2000 Dutch guilders; performance.
Deadline: December.
This competition is for composition for organ solo of approximately ten

minutes. The character and possibilities of *Schnitgerorgan* must be taken into consideration.

Periodicals

Accordeon Revue en Gitaar—Revue

57 Chrysantenstraat, Hilversum
Monthly

Bandophame (Official organ of the Netherlands Sound Society)

16 Scheldeplein, Amsterdam
Monthly

Blatter Aus Dem Clementi—Archiv Wenum

17 Nieuwe Molenweg, Wenum/Apeldoorn
Quarterly

Christelijke Muziekbode

46 Tjaerdaweg, Rinsumageest
Monthly

Delta

Netherlands Institute for International Cultural Relations
41 J.J. Viottastraat, Amsterdam
Quarterly in English; review of arts, life, and thought in the Netherlands.

Disk

Postbus 26, Te Amersfoort
Monthly

Doctor Jazz

5 van Lynden van Sandenburglaan, Utrecht
Bimonthly

Dynamite

Box 4164, Amsterdam
Monthly

Euphonia (combined with *Symphonia*)

18 Hooftweg, Hilversum
Monthly

Ex Ore Infantium

Lennards-Instituut, 16 Steegstraat, Roermond
Quarterly

Fonografiek

12 Kon. Wilhelminalaan, Postbus 26, Amersfoort
Every other week

Gaudeamus

Maastricht Male Choir, 9 Hertogsingel, Maastricht
Monthly

Gaudeamus Information

Contemporary Music Centre, Post Box 30, Bilthoven
Bimonthly; free upon request

Gregoriusblad (Magazine for the promotion of liturgical music published by the
    Netherlands St. Gregory Society)

3 Plompetorengracht, Utrecht
Bimonthly

Haagse Jazz Club

Hague Jazz Club, 7 Laan van Heldenburg, Voorburg
Monthly

Hayride-Jubilee Combinatie (Netherlands Foundation for Country and Western
    Music)

Postbus 407, Eindhoven
Monthly

Hitweek

30 Alexander Boersstraat, Amsterdam
Weekly

Huismuziek

Vereniging voor Huismuziek, 90 Schoutenkampweg, Soest
Bimonthly

J M-Krant

Jeugd en Muziek Nederland, 42 Roemer Visscherstraat, Amsterdam
Ten times a year

Jazzwereld

International Musicals N.V., 11 Leidsegracht, Amsterdam
Bimonthly

Jeugd en Muziek (Monthly of the National Federation of Belgian Youth and
   Music)

Jeugd en Muziek Nederland, 57 Jacob Obrechtstraat, Amsterdam
Irregular; 4–6 issues yearly

Journal of the Folklore Institute

Mouton & Co., Box 1132, The Hague
Three issues per year

KNF Maandblad (Offical organ of the Royal Netherlands Harmony Federation
   and Fanfare Society)

196 Groesbeekseweg, Nijmegen

Klok en Klepel

Nederlandse Klokkenspel-Vereniging, 2 Dinkelstraat, Enschede
Semiannual

Koor en Kunstleven

Harmonia-Uitgave, Hilversum
Monthly

Luister

Postbus 43, Amersfoort
Monthly

Het Maandblad

8 Cronjéstraat, Arnhem
Monthly

Mandogita (Official organ of the Netherlands Society of Mandolin Orchestras)

25 Ceintuurbaan, Amsterdam
Monthly

Mens en Melodie

10 Koudelaan, Lage Vuursche
Monthly

Musica (Military and Band Music)

J.J. Lispet, Post Box 56, Hilversum
Monthly

Muziek Expres

59 Theresiastraat, The Hague

Muziek Mercuur (Dutch Association of Record Dealers and Dealers in Music
    Instruments)

J.J. Lispet, 57 Chrysantenstraat, Hilversum
Monthly

Muziekhandel (The Society of Music Dealers and Publishers in the Netherlands)

J.J. Lispet, 57 Chrysantenstraat, Hilversum
Monthly

Nashville-Sound

G97 Laan van Vollenhove, Zeist

Ons Erfdeel (The general Netherlands trimonthly cultural review)

Frits Niessen, 1 Kerkstraat, Raamsdonkdorf Nb
Quarterly

Ons Klavier (Official organ of the technicians involved in the music instrument
    industry)

12 Karl Marxstraat, Alkmaar
Bimonthly

Opera

De Nederlandse Opera Stichting, Stadsschouwburg, Amsterdam
Six per year

Opmaat (Chronicle of the Brabant Orchestra)

Stichting Vrienden van Het Brabants Orkest van Poll en Suykerbuyk, 7
    Molenstraat, Roosendaal
Ten times a year

The Organ Yearbook (Journal for the Players and Historians of Keyboard
    Instruments)

Uitgeverij Frits Knuf, 52 Jan Kuykenstraat, Amsterdam

Organist en Eredienst (Monthly of the Strict-Calvinist Organist Society)

1 Zwanenburg, s' Heer Hendrikskinderen
Monthly

Het Orgelblad

Postbus 5063, Scheveningen

Philips Music Herald

Philips' Phonographic Industries, Baarn
Quarterly

Plateau (Official organ of the record dealers)

Fonorama N.V., Postbus 26, Amersfoort
Eleven issues per year

Platen Wereld

Postbus 26, Amersfoort

Pop-Foto/Teenbeat/Tuney Tunes

Muziek Expres N.V., 59–61–63 Theresiastraat, The Hague
Monthly

De Praestant (Trimonthly periodical for the promotion of interest in organ literature in the Netherlands)

70 hs. Stadhouderskade, Amsterdam
Trimonthly

Preludium (Organ of the Netherlands Society of Friends of the Concertgebouw)

51 Amundsenweg, Amsterdam
10 issues a year

Pyramide (Periodical for Music Education)

46 Lobelia Laan, The Hague
Bimonthly

St. Caecilia (Monthly for Woodwind Musicians)

Box 1, Purmurend
Monthly

Samenklank (Organ of the Royal Netherlands Musicians' Society)

66 Vondelstraat, Amsterdam
10 issues a year

Script (Brochure of the Congresgebouw and the Resident Orchestra)

10 Churchillplein, The Hague

Signal (Bulletin of the Council of the Federation for Dutch folksong)

17 Profetenlaan, Nijmegen
Trimonthly

Sonorum Speculum (Mirror of musical life in the Netherlands)

Donemus, 51 Jacob Obrechtstraat, Amsterdam-Z
Quarterly, free on request
This periodical contains documentation of new works by Dutch composers and details of performances of Dutch works throughout the world, together with articles covering Holland's musical life in all its aspects. Published by the Donemus Foundation (see above) with the support of the Ministry of Arts, *Sonorum Speculum* has as its chief editor Dr. Jos Wouters, prominent head of the Music Department of Radio Nederland and President of the Netherlands Committee of the International Music Council. Articles by well-known Dutch

musicians and critics appear in English and German, side by side, two columns to a page. Very often, extensive musical examples are reprinted in the magazine, sometimes from works not yet published. Regularly, a list of new compositions added to the Donemus catalog is included. In addition, *Sonorum Speculum* offers a chronicle of new music performed in the interim between the appearance of the previous issue and the current one. The publication is the delight of contemporary Dutch musicians.

Tijdschrift van de Vereniging voor Nederlandse Muziekgeschiedenis (Review of the Society for Dutch Musical History)

10 Nieuwe Weg, Lochem
Semiannually
This is the scholarly publication of the Dutch musicologists.

Basel

St. Gall

Zurich

Einsiedeln

Neuchâtel   Bern   Lucerne

Fribourg   Thun
Interlaken

Lausanne
Vevey Gstaad
Montreux

Geneva

Sion

Ascona

Lugano

Switzerland

Switzerland

Precision is the first clue to an understanding of the Swiss; business is next. Whatever they do, they do with precision, with elegance, and with style. When the operation can also be profitable, they double their efforts. Music in Switzerland is a business, a well-organized enterprise. It has always been that way.

In the early Middle Ages, the monastery of St. Gallen in northeast Switzerland was one of the chief centers of Gregorian chant. Later, in order to appeal to more of the people, the monasteries of Einsiedeln, Rheinau, and St. Gallen staged numerous performances of liturgical plays—including the famous Passion Play—in the vernacular rather than Latin. Since the fifteenth century, musical instruction has been an accepted part of the public school curriculum, and even today, boys and girls of the cantons often participate in musical events of significance.

Organ building and organ playing became a specialty of the Swiss in the sixteenth century. At this time, too, the famous theorist Glareanus (1488–1563), wrote his treatise, *Dodecachordon,* in which he extended the traditional eight church modes to twelve, thus anticipating the concept of twelve (dodeca) chromatic notes within the octave. In the eighteenth century, the philosopher Jean-Jacques Rousseau (1712–1778), earned his living in Geneva as a musical copyist, and later he wrote French comic operas in the style of the successful Italian opera buffa that he admired so much. Émile Jacques Dalcroze (1865–1950) introduced a *solfège* as well as a rhythmic method in 1892 at the Conservatory in Geneva; it is still in use throughout the Western world today. At all times the Swiss have displayed a special affinity for music. Rather than the visual arts or literature, music rates highest with the Swiss.

Any discussion of Switzerland must take into account the variety of regions and people that together comprise the Swiss nation. The diverse cantons exist in perpetual competition, each one with its neighbors. Emphasizing their differences are the three languages spoken by inhabitants of the German, French, and Italian regions of the country. Most people are bilingual. Within each large city, multiple dialects as well as two or more languages are spoken by a high percentage of the populace. In the German section, for example, the Swiss language, *Schweizerdeutsch*—a spoken language, not a written one—is learned first in school; German is used later as the more formal lecture language. All government publications are in three languages. No problem here when opera is given in the original!

Religious differences unfortunately prove more troublesome. Switzerland is, after all, the birthplace of John Calvin, a prominent leader of Protestantism, the state religion. Catholics cannot be professors in Zurich and by the same token, Protestants cannot become professors in Fribourg! We won't say the posts are evenly divided, but everything and everyone is in its proper place. Typically, as a result of municipal chauvinism, individual cities occasionally assume the role of patron in their subsidy of cultural projects. Businessmen will support a particular program that might otherwise be impossible to sustain. It would be hard to find a parallel for the Swiss company known as Migros, where their premiums—instead of being sets of dishes or transistor radios—are tickets to concert series given in the local concert hall. Equally unlikely is the spectacle of the president of this organization awarding a prize for the best contemporary composition in the field of chamber music, with the result obtained by the familiar democratic process: a vote by the audience after auditioning the three compositions judged best by a combined committee of businessmen and artists. Since they are a cooperative, not a profit-making organization, what would normally be profits paid to stockholders is instead used for cultural activities for the benefit of all the people of Switzerland. Migros spends one percent of its retail volume on culture.

Swissair, too, gets into the act. Leave for Vienna on that airline, and at the same time you select your seat on the plane, you may also choose your seat at the world-famous Vienna Opera House. The seating plan is available for your consultation at the desk. To the Swiss, music represents another commodity that they can offer to both their own citizens and tourists. A multitude of festivals attracts visitors all year long, whether it be the June festival in Zurich, the fall festival in Lucerne, the Fastnacht that transforms Basel into a Renaissance city three days and nights in February, or the folkloristic performances by Alpine musicians in the high mountain districts during August.

The most important urban centers of music in Switzerland today are Zurich, Basel, Berne, Lucerne, Wintherthur, and St. Gall in the German area; Geneva, Lausanne, Fribourg, Bienne, and Neuchâtel in the French region; Locarno and Lugano in the Italian cantons. Choral singing, especially in men's groups, is popular throughout the country. According to Fodor's Herbert Kubly, in Zurich alone we find 53 men's choruses, 10 concert halls, and 560 teachers of music! The first musical organization established in Switzerland—again in Zurich—was associated with this tradition of choral singing. This group, the Schweizerische Musikgesellschaft, established in 1808 by Beethoven's friend,

Hans Georg Nägeli, helped to make music a significant part of the national culture.

Their superior educational system has produced more top performers than composers. Among the latter, we can mention Arthur Honegger (1892–1955), who spent most of his productive life in France, Othmar Schoeck (1886–1957), Frank Martin (b. 1890), and Ernest Bloch (1880–1959), the last named better known for his work in Jewish liturgical music. By and large, the Swiss are a conservative people and their musicians do not appear overly receptive to the experiments of the avant-garde. Schoenberg and Berg are nevertheless important influences on a few composers, particularly Wladimir Vogel (b. 1906), who takes *Sprechstimme* a step further than Berg himself by utilizing it for chorus as well as for soloists. Jazz elements penetrate the works of Rolf Lieberman (b. 1910), the Zurich-born composer and conductor who recently left to become director of the Paris Opera while still retaining a top post at the Hamburg Opera. Among the younger composers, those who seem more responsive to the musical language of Webern and Boulez are Robert Suter (b. 1919), Jacques Wildberger (b. 1922), and Klaus Huber (b. 1924). Associated with the contemporary music group at Darmstadt, Germany, they bring an international flavor to their compositions.

The Swiss have shrewdly managed to remain neutral throughout two disastrous global conflicts. While intermittent destruction and devastation has been the rule for most of the countries surrounding them, they have been able to continue uninterrupted on the path of peace and prosperity. For years their banks, museums, libraries, and collections have grown and flourished to emerge in time as among the finest in Europe. Because of the security offered them here, many extremely wealthy individuals and foundations have established themselves in Switzerland.

These comments lead naturally to a final word about private collections: they are among the best in the world. From the famous Bodmer collection of Beethoveniana in Geneva to the remarkable private library of Erwin Jacobi in Zurich and the treasures of Anthony van Hoboken in Ascona, the musical resources of Switzerland defy the imagination. Each of these collections can be consulted if a scholar makes his intentions known to the owner sufficiently well in advance of his visit.

Guides and Services

Swiss National Tourist Office
42 Talacker, CH-8023 Zurich   Tel: (051) 23 57 13

The Swiss Center (USA)
608 Fifth Avenue, New York, N.Y. 10020   Tel: (212) 757-5944

The Swiss National Tourist Office(USA)
661 Market Street, San Francisco, California 94105   Tel: (415) 362-2260

Summer in Switzerland and *Winter in Switzerland: Events* (in English)
Appears twice a year and includes a diary of events taking place throughout Switzerland for the entire year. This publication is available gratis at the offices listed above. It contains information about music festivals, music master courses, cultural weeks, major theater, film, and open-air performances, art exhibitions, local festivals and folklore, trade fairs, international congresses, seminars, language courses, and sporting events.
     For musicians, musicologists, and amateurs, two organizations should prove helpful. They are:

Association des musiciens suisses
Avenue du Grammont 11 bis, 1000 Lausanne   Tel: (021) 26 63 71

International Musicological Society
P.O. Box 588, Basel, CH-4001
(See Basel, *Musical Organizations*)

For an excellent recent book on Switzerland, see Jonathan Steinberg's *Why Switzerland?* (Cambridge University Press, 1976).

NATIONAL HOLIDAYS

January	1	New Year's Day
	2	Barzelistag (Zurich only)
March	19	St. Joseph's Day (6 cantons)
	*	Good Friday
April	*	Easter Monday
May	*	Ascension
	*	Whit Monday
June	*	Corpus Christi
	29	SS. Peter and Paul
August	1	National Day (half day)
November	1	All Saints' Day
December	8	Immaculate Conception
	25	Christmas
	26	St. Stephen's Day

* = movable

GENEVA   Tel. prefix: (022)

Geneva is several cities in one: an international city, a commercial city, a tourist's city, and an old city. To the world, Geneva represents the headquarters of perhaps a dozen world health and security organizations and for this reason is constantly filled with the widest variety of foreigners, many of whom reside there for a period of several years. To the well-heeled European and American tourists, Geneva with its lake is a playground, both summer and winter. Of course, until recently there was the added security of numbered bank accounts.

To the casual traveler and even to students, Geneva is watch country and a good place to shop. Despite the natives' claim that it's not formal, Geneva is still not the place to walk in hotpants or bikinis, nor would you attend the opera here in Levis. The old city in the hills is delightful and charming and beckons everyone, but is still not what one calls to mind when thinking of Geneva. The real citizens of this town regard themselves more or less as Rousseau did two hundred years ago—they are citizens of Geneva, not citizens of Switzerland.

With the good life come the proper accessories, and Geneva can lay claim to a fine conservatory and an excellent opera house modeled after Garnier's Opéra in Paris (and rebuilt to these specifications even after the disastrous fire of 1951). Its Orchestre de la Suisse Romande, which achieved world renown under the late conductor, Ernest Ansermet, performs at Victoria Hall. The Hotel de Ville also offers musical attractions, but music is not the reason most people go to Geneva. It is simply ancillary to their visit. Geneva, third largest city after Zurich and Basel, with a population around 360,000, is not usually a musician's favorite.

Guides and Services

Office du Tourisme de Genève   Tel: 32 66 25

La Semaine à Genève

Like every Swiss city of appreciable size, Geneva has a weekly guide obtainable at most major newsstands and hotels. This brochure includes information on entertainment, museums, libraries, shops, and international organizations as well as other useful material. All information appears in three languages: French, German, and English.

Opera Houses and Concert Halls

Grand Théâtre de Genève

Place Neuve   Tel: 26 43 60

Mailing Address: 11 boulevard du Théâtre, 1211 Geneva

Season: September to June; closed holidays.

Box Office Hours: open, depending on presentation, on day of performance from 10:00 AM to noon and 3:00 PM to 7:00 PM.

Customary Dress: tuxedo or evening dress for galas; otherwise street dress, but tie for men always necessary.

Opera, ballet, concerts, and occasionally plays are performed here.

In 1766–67, Geneva's first theater opened its season with plays by Molière and Voltaire and an opera, *Isabelle et Gertrude,* by Favart and Grétry. The following year, possibly with Rousseau's "help," the house burned down. Although a new theater was built in 1782, it was not until almost a hundred years later, in 1879, that the Grand Théâtre, a replica of Charles Garnier's Paris Opéra, was finally constructed. The structure was completed with the aid of a grant from the Duke of Brunswick, who lived his last years in Geneva. The first performance in the new theater on October 2, 1879, was Rossini's *William Tell;* subsequently *Carmen* and *Faust* were among the many contemporary operas presented.

After World War I, with the decline of interest in opera, Ernest Ansermet led the Orchestre de la Suisse Romande in numerous performances of opera in concert form here. Slowly opera returned to favor. Then, on May 1, 1951, at a rehearsal of *Die Walküre,* as the stagehands tried out a new type of flamethrower, a fire broke out that almost destroyed the entire theater.

Plagued with difficulties of various kinds, those involved in the reconstruction of the house were often close to losing faith that they would ever again have an opera house. During the next few years, opera was presented in the Grand Casino. (Incidentally, in this city all operas are performed in their original language.) Finally, after much effort and many months of work supported by more than two and a half million dollars voted in a public referendum, on December 10, 1962, the magnificent Grand Théâtre on the Place Neuve opened with a splendid new production of Verdi's *Don Carlo.* Today the opera house is one of the foremost in Europe.

Conservatoire de Musique (Concert Hall)

Place Neuve   Tel: 25 00 71

Radio Genève: Studio de Radiodiffusion à Genève de la Radio Suisse Romande

66 boulevard Carl-Vogt   Tel: 25 43 00

Season: entire year.
Seating Capacity: 350 in concert hall.

Victoria Hall

5 promenade du Pin   Tel: 26 72 11, ext. 442
Box Office Mailing Address: rue du General Dufour (although location is actually
    Grand-Passage-Epis d'or)
Season: entire year.
Hours: Monday to Saturday, no specific hours.
Standing Room: available only if house is filled to capacity.
Customary Dress: street clothes.
Presentations are under the direction of the Service des Spectacles et Concerts
de la Ville de Genève. Concerts, jazz, and folk music presented here.

Libraries and Museums

Bibliothèque Publique et Universitaire [Ben. 18]

Promenade des Bastions   Tel: 25 62 40
Hours: Monday to Friday, 9:00 AM to 10:00 PM; Saturday, 9:00 AM to 1:00 PM and
    2:00 PM to 7:00 PM. During school vacations hours are: Monday to Friday,
    9:00 AM to noon and 2:00 PM to 7:00 PM; Saturday, 9:00 AM to 12:10 PM.
    Closed August. For access, apply to guard desk of reading room.

Conservatoire de Musique, Bibliothèque [Ben. 19]

Place Neuve   Tel: 25 00 71
Hours: Monday, Wednesday, Friday, 2:00 PM to 4:00 PM; Thursday and
    Saturday, 10:00 AM to noon. Closed fifteen days at Christmas and Easter;
    closed July and August.

Musée Jean-Jacques Rousseau

Bibliothèque Publique et Universitaire
Promenade des Bastions   Tel: 25 62 40
Hours: Thursday, 2:00 PM to 4:00 PM; Sunday, 11:00 AM to noon and 2:00 PM to
    4:00 PM.
This museum was founded in 1916 by the J. J. Rousseau Society. Rousseau, who
made his living while a young man as a musical copyist, was a citizen of Geneva,
not Switzerland.

Musée d'instruments anciens de musique

23 rue Lefort   Tel: 46 95 65; 24 58 61
Hours: Tuesday, 3:00 PM to 7:00 PM; Thursday, 10:00 AM to noon; Friday, 8:00
    PM to 10:00 PM.

Instruments are played during guided tours. Concerts of early music are given in the museum's concert hall.

Musée d'art et d'histoire
2 rue Charles Galland   Tel: 25 92 36
Hours: Tuesday to Sunday, 10:00 AM to noon; 2:00 PM to 6:00 PM; Monday, 2:00 PM to 6:00 PM.
Musical instruments are in the Section Historique.

Musée et Institut d'ethnographie (Ethnographical Museum and Institute)
65-67 boulevard Carl Vogt   Tel: 24 88 44
Hours: Tuesday to Sunday, 10:00 AM to noon, 2:00 PM to 5:00 PM; Friday, 8:00 PM to 10:00 PM in addition.

Conservatories and Schools

Conservatoire de Musique de Genève
Place Neuve   Tel: 25 00 71; 26 31 20

Cours de musicologie de l'université de Genève
Rue de Candolle

Institut Jacques Dalcroze
44 rue Terrassière
Of special interest are the following publications:
    H. Brochet, *Le Conservatoire de Musique á Genève, 1835–1935* (Geneva, 1936)
    H. Gagnebin, *Une Notice sur la Bibliothèque du Conservatoire* (Geneva, 1935)

University of Geneva
1211 Geneva 4
The University offers seventeen exchange scholarships to students from different countries including the United States. The scholar has the choice of his field of advanced study; he must have acquired his B.A. and have given indication of an ability to carry on independent research.

Summer Schools

Music Holidays in Geneva
Address: (Conservatoire, above)
Like Geneva University, which gives a French-language course for foreigners each summer, the Conservatory of Music organizes master classes in piano, violin, and flute offered by different prominent musicians each year. During the

summer, concerts are also given by orchestras such as the Orchestre de la Suisse Romande.

Musical Organizations

European Association of Music Festivals
122 rue de Lausanne

Federation of International Music Competitions
Palais Eynard
4 rue de la Croix-Rouge, CH-1204

Jeunesses Musicales of Switzerland
66 boulevard Carl Vogt

The Business of Music

Music Dealers

Au Menestrel, Maison de la Musique
    15 quai de l'Isle, CH-1204   Tel: 24 96 77

Champion
    8 rue Versonnex

Sautier & Jaeger
    12 place de la Fusterie

Concert Managers

M. Casetti-Giovanna
Bureau de Concerts, Spectacles et Conférences
    3 rue de l'Evêché   Tel: 24 03 80

ZURICH   Tel. prefix: (051)

Zurich is a great city. Wagner thought so years ago and we still think so today. The largest of the Swiss cities, it is also the richest, with more millionaires among its half-million people than are found in any other place of similar size in the world. It's a safe city, as are most of the urban centers in Switzerland; despite the fact that every male has a rifle in his home and regularly engages in rifle practice in order to be prepared for mobilization on twenty-four-hours' notice, very few murders are committed.

Just as Geneva appears French, so Zurich seems German. The architecture, the street signs, the inclinations of the people—and of course their language, except for the *Schweizerdeutsch* dialect—correspond to those found in Germany. Their private collections of both art and literature are extraordinarily fine, and their museums rank with the best in the world.

If their local performers are not always top-notch, their facilities are excellent and, when necessary, they import the foremost foreign artists. The magnificent opera house on Bellevueplatz and Sechselautenplatz near the lake reeks of *fin de siècle*. The dignity of their Tonhalle bespeaks the integrity of its sponsors and backers. The zeal with which the Allgemeine Musikgesellschaft Zurich prepares its annual *Neujahrsblatt* on January 2 (as it has done every year since 1815) reveals the position accorded to music in this city. Organ building, too, is important in Switzerland, and the Metzler factory near Zurich as well as the Kuhn plant at Mennedorf are significant European centers of this craft. Choirs, both male and mixed, play an active role in musicmaking here. Of course it's the June Festival that rates highest among foreigners' favorites, but native Zürchers get music year round and they show an intense interest in what is provided for them.

Guides and Services

Verkehrsverein Zurich (Tourist Office)
15 Bahnhofplatz, CH-8023   Tel: 25 67 00
Zurich Official Weekly Bulletin, in English, is available at most major hotels and newsstands. The *Chronique de Zurich* is issued monthly by the Zurich Tourist Office, located in the main rail station. It is an excellent guide to concerts, theaters, and exhibits.

Opera Houses and Concert Halls

Tonhalle
7 Claridenstrasse   Tel: 36 15 81
Mailing Address: 1 Gotthardstrasse
Season: September 1 to July 1. Closed Christmas and other holidays.

Box Office: Billetkasse der Tonhallegesellschaft.

Hours: Monday to Friday, 9:00 AM to 12:30 PM and 3:00 PM to 6:00 PM; Saturday, 9:00 AM to 12:30 PM. No standing room.

Authorized Ticket Agencies: Pianohaus Jecklin, Pfauen; Hug & Co., 28 Limmatquai; Kuoni Travel Agency, 7 Bahnhofplatz.

Customary Dress: Men, dark suits; during June Festival, men wear tuxedos and women cocktail dresses.

Although most concerts take place in the concert and recital halls of the Tonhalle, Zurich has a number of other, less central—and less popular—concert halls. There are five regular concert cycles:

1. Concerts organized by the Tonhalle Gesellschaft. This organization, founded in 1868, has its own orchestra, the Tonhalle Orchestra in Zurich, comprised of 175 musicians. They offer 63 orchestral concerts and 27 chamber concerts annually.

   Programs are available in advance from Tonhalle Gesellschaft, 1 Gotthardstrasse, CH-8002. Tel: 36 15 81

2. Concerts called the Klubhaus-Konzerte. Offering about fifteen concerts a season, this group presents foreign orchestras and ensembles. Programs are available from Klaus Menzel, Postfach 483, CH-8022. Tel: 25 33 88

3. The Zürcher Kammerorchester under its director Edmond de Stoutz offers about seventeen concerts a year. Programs may be obtained at 55 Kreuzstrasse, CH-8032. Tel: 34 17 37

4. The Collegium Musicum Zürich under the direction of Dr. Paul Sacher presents six concerts a season. Programs are available at the Konzertgesellschaft, 2 Steinwiesstrasse, CH-8032.

5. The Camerata Zürich, a chamber orchestra under the direction of Rato Tschupp, performs six concerts a year. Programs are available at Postfach A 177, CH-8034. Tel: 34 11 10

Opernhaus

Theaterplatz   Tel: 32 69 20; 32 69 22

Mailing Address: 1 Schillerstrasse

Season: September until the end of June, including June Festival. Annual Closing: Swiss Thanksgiving Day (third Sunday in September), Christmas Eve and Day, Good Friday, Easter Sunday, Whitsunday.

Box Office: see mailing address.

Hours: daily 10:00 AM to 7:00 PM; Sunday 10:00 AM to noon and 3:00 PM to 5:00 PM.

Authorized Ticket Agencies: Kuoni Travel Agency, 7 Bahnhofplatz; Haffner Travel Agency, 339 Schaffhausestrasse.

Seating Capacity: 1200.

Customary Dress: Formal attire not necessary.

Opera, operetta, and ballet offered here. Check local paper for time.

The Opera House, founded in 1834 and given the name "Aktientheater," was destroyed by fire in 1890. Reopened on October 1, 1891, as the "Stadttheater," it has been called "Opernhaus Zürich" only since 1964. The Opera functions with its own repertory company and the assistance of guest artists. Operetta, musicals, and ballet are presented in this house. The Tonhalle Orchester Zürich (see above) serves the opera company as well as the Tonhalle.

Städtisches Podium
Stadthaus   Tel: 29 58 11
The City Hall (Stadthaus) of Zurich organizes a cycle of ten chamber concerts annually with programs devoted principally to Swiss works performed by young artists.

Libraries and Museums

Schweizerisches Musik-Archiv, formerly Zentral Schweizerischer Tonkunst (Swiss Music Archive) [Ben. 42]
82 Bellariastrasse   Tel: 45 77 00
Hours: Monday to Friday, 9:00 AM to 12:30 PM, 1:30 PM to 3:30 PM.
This organization is the Music Information Center of Switzerland.

Zentralbibliothek (or Kantons- Stadt- und Univer. itätsbibliothek) [Ben. 43]
6 Zähringerplatz   Tel: 32 14 00; 34 35 15
Hours: open weekdays. Closed ten days in September.
The autograph of Brahms's Fourth Symphony may be seen here.

Library of Dr. Erwin Jacobi (Private) [Ben. 39]
29 Riedgrabenweg   Tel: 46 48 18
Hours: by appointment only.
It is advisable to write well in advance of your arrival in Zurich. Dr. Jacobi is often away. As of 1975, most of Dr. Jacobi's library will belong to the Zentralbibliothek (see above) and will be housed there.

Musikwissenschaftliches Seminar der Universität (Musicology Department of Zurich University) [Ben. 41]
8 Florhofgasse   Tel: 34 53 33
Hours: Tuesday to Friday; about thirty hours weekly. Closed school vacations
    and three weeks in September. Open all year to keyholders.

Konservatorium und Musikhochschule, Bibliothek (Library of Conservatory and Music School) [Ben. 40]

6 Florhofgasse   Tel: 32 89 55
Hours: Tuesday to Friday afternoons. Closed school vacations.
For access apply to school secretary.

Schweizerisches Landesmuseum (Swiss National Museum)
2 Museumstrasse   Tel: 25 79 35
Hours: Tuesday to Sunday, 10:00 AM to noon; 2:00 PM to 5:00 PM; (October to
April; only until 4:00 PM; on Sunday to 5:00 PM).
Free access. Inquire about instruments at office of secretary.

Wesendonck Villa (Museum Rietberg)
15 Gablerstrasse   Tel: 25 45 28
Hours: open Tuesday to Friday, 10:00 AM to noon, 2:00 PM to 6:00 PM; Saturday
and Sunday, 10:00 AM to noon, and 2:00 PM to 5:00 PM; Wednesday also
8:00 PM to 10:00 PM.
This contains the foremost collection of Chinese sculpture in Europe as well as
important collections of art from all Asia. Significant to music lovers who
should note that this is the historic Wesendonck villa, home of Otto and
Mathilde Wesendonck, Wagner's hosts when he composed parts of *Siegfried* and
Tristan.

Of special interest to those investigating the musical life of Zurich are the
following publications:
    Martin Hurlimann, *Musiker Hss: Zeugnisse des Zürcher Musiklebens* (Zurich,
        1969).
    O. Schneider, "Zürcher Musikleben," in *Schweizerische Musikzeitung* XC,
        1950 (218-226).
    Rudolf Schoch, *100 Jahre Tonhalle Zürich* (Zurich, 1968).
    This book is a history of the city's musical life since 1613.
    Willi Schuh et al. *Schweizer Musiker-Lexikon* (Zurich, 1964).
    This volume is a comprehensive dictionary of Swiss musicians.
    Music in Switzerland, a brochure published by Pro Helvetia, Information
        and Press Service, CH 8001 Zurich.

Conservatories and Schools

Konservatorium und Musikhochschule Zürich
6 Florhofgasse   Tel: 32 89 55

Musikakademie Zürich
52 Florastrasse

This school offers courses for nonprofessionals, who, if they desire to pursue a career, transfer to the Hochschule (see above).

University of Zurich

This university offers exchange scholarships, usually two to a country, to students from several different nations, including the United States. For information write to the Institute of International Education, 809 United Nations Plaza, New York, N.Y. 10017.

Here are two suggestions for those looking into summer courses or attending some of the festivals. The following two hostels might be worth a visit:

Jugendherberge (Youth Hostel)
114 Mutschellenstrasse   Tel: 45 35 44
Open all year round.

Touristenlager (Tourist Hostel)
118 Limmatstrasse   Tel: 42 38 00
Open May to September; for reservations write Quartieramt, P.O.B., 8027 Zurich.

Internationale Meisterkurse für Musik

Postfach 647   Tel: 28 52 28
Location of classes: Muraltengut, 203 Seestrasse   Tel. (during season): 45 31 44
No degrees granted.
Course of Study: one or two weeks from mid-May through July.
Prerequisites: admission by audition; a limited number of people will also be admitted to all courses as potential members of the audience; active musicians have priority.

The course is an opportunity for gifted young artists to work with masters of their profession who are internationally renowned. They may thus obtain an appraisal of their standing and advice on their future work in order to assist them in reaching their goals. Recent faculty has included Jennie Tourel, Geza Anda, Ernst Haefliger, Nathan Milstein, Pierre Fournier, and others. For housing accommodations, write the Zurich Association for Promoting Tourism, 15 Bahnhofplatz, 8023 Zurich.

International Opera Center (Internationales Opernstudio)

Opernhaus, 1 Schillerstrasse   Tel: 32 69 20
Course of Study: approximately thirty-eight weeks during the regular season of the Zurich Opera Company.
Degree Granted: certificate of achievement.
Prerequisites: completed vocal study so that a professional operatic engagement is possible after one, or at most two, seasons in the studio; entrance exams and auditions held in various countries.

Areas of Instruction: individual operatic coaching, operatic ensemble, stylistic interpretation, opera dramatics, speech and enunciation, regular attendance at rehearsals and performances of Zurich Opera House.

Housing Provisions: the administration helps members in finding rooms with Swiss families.

Write to above address for catalog. The parent organization here is the Opernhaus Zürich.

Musical Organizations

Allgemeine Musikgesellschaft Zürich (AMG)

6 Zähringerplatz, third floor   Tel: 32 14 00

Hours: Monday to Friday 2:00 PM to 6 PM; Saturday 2:00 PM to 5:00 PM. Closed holidays.

No special credentials necessary.

Founded in 1812, the AMG exercised a decisive influence on concert life in Zurich during the nineteenth century. It organized subscription concerts under their own and foreign conductors (Richard Wagner, 1850–1855). In 1868, the Tonhallegesellschaft assumed the role of leadership in concert life. Two duties are now assumed by the AMG: 1. The administration and the cultivation of the library of the AMG, located in the music department of the Zentralbibliothek (see *Libraries*); 2. The editing and publishing of an annual "Neujahrsblatt."

Association Européenne des Directeurs des Conservatoires

6 Florhofgasse

Association Suisse de Pédagogie Musicale

6 Sophienstrasse

Union Suisse des Artistes Musiciens

35 Talacker

Schweizerisches Musik-Archiv (Swiss Music Information Center)

82 Bellariastrasse   Tel: 45 77 00

Societies

International Federation of Musicians

60 Kreuzstrasse   Tel: 47 45 67

Musikverband der Stadt Zürich (Musical Union of City of Zurich)

40 Zypressenstrasse   Tel: 52 49 36

Musik der Verkehrsbetriebe Zürich
Wydenstrasse   Tel: 39 80 47

Schweizerische Musiker-Verband
11 Talstrasse   Tel: 25 24 11

Schweizerische Musikpädagogischer Verband
376 Forschstrasse   Tel: 53 17 52

Musikverein Albisrieden
6 Diggelmannstrasse   Tel: 54 92 77

Evangelische Musikkorps der Stadt Zürich
8 Freyastrasse   Tel: 23 07 04

Harmonie Zürich-Unterstrasse
118 Forchstrasse   Tel: 53 81 76

Schweizerische Gesellschaft der Urheber und Verleger (SUISA)
82 Bellariastrasse   Tel: 45 77 00

Schweizerische Vereinigung für Hausmusik
25 Burglistrasse   Tel: 36 37 64

Schweizerische Berufsdirigenten Verband (SBV)
132 Fronwaldstrasse   Tel: 57 26 63

Studio Zürich
20-22 Brunnenhofstrasse   Tel: 60 07 00

The Business of Music

Music Dealers

Hug & Co. (with two branches)
    4 Füsslistrasse   Tel: 25 69 40
    26-28 Limmatquai   Tel: 32 68 50

Inquire here about the Hug company's remarkable private instrument collection. Available in this store are pocket metronomes. Hug & Co. are Switzerland's foremost music merchants.

Otto Rindlisbacher
    23-26 Dubsstrasse

For over a hundred years, this family has sold pianos and early instruments including harpsichords, clavichords, and spinets.

Jecklin-Pianos
    Pfauen, 30 Rämistrasse   Tel: 45 37 20

Music and Arts
    Tobelhofstrasse   Tel: 47 65 22

Musical AG
    11 Oetenbachgasse   Tel: 27 43 62; 23 13 44

Musikhaus Bertschinger
    32 Hottingerstrasse   Tel: 47 37 09

Music Publishers

Musik Verlag zum Pelikan
    22 Bellerivestrasse   Tel: 32 57 90

Musik-Verlag Polyton Lutz Harteck
    10 Geranienstrasse   Tel: 55 02 04

Concert Managers

Klubhaus Konzerte
    7 Zürichbergstrasse

Konzertdirektion Klaus Menzel
    Postfach 483

Konzertbureau Schlaepfer
    44 Hottingerstrasse   Tel: 47 18 10

Konzertagentur Hug & Co.
    28 Limmatquai

BASEL (BASLE)   Tel. prefix: (061)

Even earlier than Berne, Basel is mentioned in the history books of the fourth century as a Roman station with the name Basilia, meaning royal residence. Six hundred years later it belonged to Burgundy and shortly thereafter became part of the German Empire. Its unhappy association with the house of Hapsburg ended in 1501 when it joined the Swiss Confederation.

Like Cologne (see *The Music Guide to Austria and Germany*), Basel is a Rhenish city. Straddling the Rhine with cultural, commercial, and intellectual centers on one bank and industrial areas on the other, Basel is a thriving trade center. Almost on the borders of both France and Germany, it is, like Geneva, a thoroughly cosmopolitan city—but for different reasons. Whereas Geneva plays host to many international organizations and shelters their personnel within its borders, Basel owes its sophistication to its geographical location.

Each of the Swiss cities is intensely independent and different from its neighbors. None wants to conform to a distinctly national type. As an example, there are four universities with departments of musicology in Switzerland: Zurich, Basel, Geneva, and Fribourg. Each calls its Master's degree by a different name. It is the considered opinion of specialists that the department and the library at Basel are the best the country has to offer. There is no federal department of education. Each canton must subsidize its own cultural programs, and each canton has its own university. Unlike other Europeans, the Swiss have just begun federal assistance. Two new institutions, the Technical Universities in Lausanne and in Zurich, both receive their support from the state. The University of Basel, founded by Pope Pius II in 1460, became known as a seat of humanism through the work of Erasmus in the sixteenth century. More recently, it has achieved fame through two alumni, the historian, Jacob Burckhardt, and the philosopher, Friedrich Nietzsche.

Basel's Kunstmuseum has one of the finest art collections in Switzerland. Unfortunately, there is no opera house in this city. The Basler Stadttheater is used for both theater and opera.

Guides and Services

Verkehrsverein (Tourist Office)
2 Blumenrain   Tel: 24 38 35

Basel Weekly Bulletin (in English)
Available at major hotels and newsstands.

Opera Houses and Concert Halls

Basler Theater
1 Theaterstrasse   Tel: 25 92 40
Season: mid-September to end of June; closed six weeks for vacation, also
    Christmas and Easter. Opera, operetta, plays, ballet, pop concerts.
Box Office: Stadttheater   Tel: 24 19 65
              Komödie   Tel: 23 79 75

Hours: Monday to Saturday, 10:00 AM to 12:30 PM and 3:00 PM to 6:45 PM; Sunday, 10:00 AM to 12:30 PM.
Seating Capacity: Stadttheater, 1150; Komödie, 372.
Customary Dress: as you like.
Unlike Zurich or Geneva, Basel does not have an opera house. Different halls of the Stadtcasino are occasionally the sites of performances.

Libraries and Museums

Öffentliche Bibliothek der Universität Basel [Ben. 5]
20 Schönbeinstrasse   Tel: 25 22 50
Hours: Monday, Tuesday, Thursday, 9:00 AM to 10:00 PM; Wednesday and Friday, 9:00 AM to 7:00 PM; Saturday, 9:00 AM to 5:00 PM. Closed for vacation from about July 15 to August 1. Apply to Director for admission.
Theory, history, twentieth-century literature on Swiss music history; musical treatises and liturgical manuscripts of the late medieval period; manuscripts of Liederbücher of the sixteenth century; Lucas Sarasin collection of manuscripts of eighteenth-century vocal and instrumental music; Edgar Refardt collection of materials on Basel music history; library of the Schweizerische Musikforschende Gesellschaft (Swiss Society for Musical Research).
This library is the country's most important music library.

Musikwissenschaftliches Institut (formerly Seminar) der Universität Basel [Ben. 4]
27 Petersgraben   Tel: 23 55 23
Hours: Monday to Saturday.
Apply to Secretary.

Musik-Akademie der Stadt Basel (formerly Musikschule und Konservatorium), Bibliothek [Ben. 3]
6 Leonhardsstrasse   Tel: 24 59 35, ext. 15
Hours: Monday to Friday 9:15 AM to 11:15 AM; 1:30 PM to 6:00 PM. Closed Christmas, New Year's; March 15 to April 15; July 1 to August 15; October 1 to 15.
Slight fee for nonstudents.

Historisches Museum, Sammlung alter Musikinstrumente
8 Leonhardsstrasse   Tel: 24 34 50
Hours: Sunday 10:00 AM to 12:30 PM; 2:00 PM to 5:00 PM.
The collection includes Swiss and European folk instruments; other instruments from the sixteenth to nineteenth centuries.

Conservatories and Schools

Musikakademie der Stadt Basel
4-6 Leonhardsstrasse   Tel: 23 57 22

University of Basel
1 Petersplatz
Three exchange scholarships are available to United States citizens. For information concerning qualifications and procedures write Institute of International Education, 809 United Nations Plaza, New York, N.Y. 10017. To supplement the scholarships, additional monies are offered each semester to those students who have done exceptionally well.

Musikwissenschaftliches Institut der Universität Basel(See *Libraries*)
Of special interest to those investigating the musical life of Basel are the following publications:
   W. Merian, *Basel's Musikleben im XIX Jh.* (Basel, 1920).
   W. Merian, *Gedenkschrift zum 50jährigen Bestehen der Allgemeinen Musikschule . . . Basel* (Basel, 1917).
   Ernst Lichtenharn, "Schweizerische Musikforschende Gesellschaft" in *Acta Musicologica*, XLVII (1975) 292-94.

Musical Organizations

Association Internationale des Bibliothèques Musicales, Section Suisse
Postfach 203

Société Suisse de Musicologie (Swiss Musicological Society)
25 Passwangstrasse
Mailing Address: Postfach 1561
This organization, a branch of the International Musicological Society, publishes the *Schweizerische Musikdenkmäler* (Swiss Musical Monuments), to date consisting of eight volumes; Swiss dissertations; several sets of complete works, among them those of Goudimel and Senfl; and a newsletter.

Societies

Musikpädagogische Verband (SMPV) (Music Educators Union)
53 Untern Schellenberg   Tel: 49 36 02

Musikverein Klein-Basel (Music Club)
30 Am Stausee   Tel: 41 89 15

Schweizerische Radio- und Fernseh-Gesellschaft (Swiss Radio and Television)
50 Marignanstrasse   Tel: 34 62 20

Studio Basel
2 Novarastrasse   Tel: 34 58 40

Vereinigung der Konzertgebenden Gesellschaft der Schweiz (VKGS)
(Union of Swiss Performing Societies)
18 Münsterplatz   Tel: 25 42 66

Symphony Orchestras

Basler Kammerorchester
4 Leonhardsstrasse   Tel: 23 42 52

Basler Orchester-Gesellschaft (BOG)
18 Münsterplatz   Tel: 24 42 66

The Business of Music

Pianos

Piano-Eckenstein
    48 Leonhardsgraben   Tel: 23 99 10

Concert Managers

Konzertagentur Hug & Co.
    70 Freistrasse

M. P. Gutter
    70 Freistrasse

Dealers

Musikhaus au Concert
    24 Aeschen vor Strasse   Tel: 23 11 76
Records and tickets available here.

BERNE (BERN)   Tel. prefix: (031)

Berne is a patrician city. Established on a firm footing almost a millennium ago, this is a city of well-to-do families, conservative in their thinking and dedicated to the concept of democratic and responsible government. The Bernese don't expect too many tourists and they don't go out of their way to attract them. They are always themselves, and there is no sham or hypocrisy here.

These solid citizens do not have much time for the arts. They do, however, have a fine conservatory, a splendid art museum, and the Bernische Musikgesellschaft, a society concerned with the promotion of good music. Concerts are generally given in the auditorium of the Conservatory and in the Berne Casino. On Theaterplatz, across from the Casino, is the City and University Library built between 1787 and 1792. To the south and across the Aare River, which divides this city of 170,000 people, stands the massive Swiss National Library. Built in 1929–1932, today it has over a million volumes, 25,000 maps, and 120,000 drawings and engravings.

The older part of the city preserves its medieval layout. Small wonder, for the Cathedral still dominates the landscape. On the right bank of the river is the new section, whose industries include weaving, spinning, machinery production, chocolate, and pharmaceuticals. As yet the city has no separate opera house, so operas and dramas are presented in the same theater.

On Tuesdays during the summer, *Abendmusik,* consisting of selections of sacred organ and vocal music, is offered in the Cathedral with its extraordinary 5,000-pipe organ. Berne's annual Opera Week takes place in June.

Guides and Services

Verkehrsverein (Tourist Office)
20 Bundesgasse   Tel: 22 39 51

Berner Wochenbulletin is available at major hotels and newsstands.

Opera Houses and Concert Halls

Except for the concert hall in the Conservatory (see below), and the Municipal Theater, Berne has no auditoriums exclusively for musical events. Here, as in Basel, the halls of the Casino are used when necessary.

Libraries and Museums

Stadt-und Universitätsbibliothek (including Bürgerbibliothek)
[Ben. 9]
41 Kesslergasse   Tel: 22 55 19
Hours: Monday to Saturday. Closed Easter, Christmas, New Year's.
Apply to lending office.
The Stadt-Univ. Bibliothek was founded in 1528 as a school library of the *Chorherrenstift* (Choral Foundation), another indication of the importance here of choral music. The Bürgerbibliothek, founded in 1951, contains manuscripts formerly in the Stadt-Univ. Bibliothek, a reference library for work on medieval manuscripts; there are also many bequests and family archives here.

Schweizerische Landesbibliothek (or Bibliothèque Nationale Suisse)
Musikabteilung [Ben. 8]
15 Hallwylstrasse   Tel: 61 71 11
Hours: Monday to Saturday. Closed three weeks in July, afternoons in August and September.
This library acts as an agent for the exchange of books and microfilm between Swiss and foreign libraries. Here are to be found copies of all books and pamphlets published by Swiss authors or in Switzerland since 1915, and a large number of earlier works as well. In addition, the library contains a large number of microfilms of rare and out-of-print books, collections of prints, manuscripts of recent authors (e.g., Rilke and Hesse), and materials concerning drama and the theater. It also houses a catalog of every volume in any Swiss library—from university libraries to collections in clinics and industrial firms. An efficient interlibrary loan service can generally supply books from other Swiss libraries in three or four days' time.

Musikwissenschaftliches Seminar der Universität Bern, Bibliothek
[Ben. 7]
7 Längasstrasse, first floor   Tel: 23 71 71
Hours: Monday to Saturday. Closed between semesters.

Bernisches Historisches Museum, Instrumenten Sammlung
5 Helvetiaplatz   Tel: 43 18 11
Hours: Monday, 2:00 PM to 5:00 PM; Tuesday to Saturday, 9:00 AM to noon, 2:00 PM to 5:00 PM; Sunday, 10:00 AM to noon, 2:00 PM to 5:00 PM.

Konservatorium (incorporating former Berner Musikschule),
Bibliothek [Ben. 6]
36 Kramgasse   Tel: 22 16 54

Hours: Tuesday to Friday, 10:30 AM to noon and 2:00 PM to 4:00 PM; Saturday, 10:30 AM to noon and 3:00 PM to 5:00 PM. Closed school vacations.

Conservatories and Schools

Konservatorium für Musik in Bern
36 Kramgasse   Tel: 22 62 21

University of Berne
Two exchange scholarships are offered to United States students who have received their A.B. degree and are preferably less than 35 years of age. Again, write Institute of International Education, 809 United States Plaza, New York, N.Y. 10017, for more information.

Musical Organizations

Musikalische Jugend der Schweiz (Jeunesses Musicales de Suisse)
34 Steinerstrasse, 3000 Berne   Tel: 44 37 29

Musikpädagogische Vereinigung (Music Educators Association)
7 Cacilienstrasse   Tel: 45 17 16

Studio Bern (Radio Station)
21 Schwarztorstrasse   Tel: 45 44 21

Schweizerische Arbeiter-Musik-Verband (Swiss Workers Musical Union)
Postfach 29   Tel: 51 08 75

Schweizerische Arbeitersänger-Verband (Swiss Workers Vocalists Union)
28 Waldheimstrasse   Tel: 64 62 35

The Business of Music

Music Dealers

Krompholz & Cie
    28 Spitalgasse   Tel: 22 53 11
Founded in 1855, this emporium offers everything for musicians. Pianos and

harpsichords, records, TV and radio available here as well as all kinds of instrument repairs.

Pianos

Schmidt-Flohr
    34 Marktgasse

Stringed Instrument Maker

Henry Werro
    2 Zeitglockenlaube

Dealers

Musik Muller
    22 Zeughausgasse   Tel: 22 41 34

Concert Managers

Müller & Schade AG
    6 Theaterplatz   Tel: 22 16 91

SWITZERLAND, GENERAL

Opera Houses and Concert Halls

Except for the four cities of Geneva, Zurich, Berne, and Basel, the only other major city with a concert hall is Lausanne, whose Théâtre Municipal and Palais de Beaulieu offer significant musical events fairly regularly. The concert season runs from September through May in Switzerland, with summer festivals—some large (see below) and some too small to mention—accounting for additional musicmaking during the summer months.

About twenty-five other small cities have concert halls and/or theaters.

Libraries and Museums

In addition to the libraries specifically cited below, the following cities also have music libraries worth noting: Chur, Disentis, Engelberg, Fribourg, Lucerne, Thun, and Winterthur.

Ascona (Ticino)

Private Library of Dr. Anthony van Hoboken [Ben. 2]
Casa Peschiera
By appointment only. Write well in advance.
Dr. Hoboken's Archiv für Photogramme Musikalischer Meisterhss. (Archive for Photos of Manuscripts of Musical Masterworks) is in the Musiksammlung Österreichischer National Bibliothek, 1 Augustinerstrasse, Vienna (see *Music Guide to Austria and Germany*).

Einsiedeln (Schwyz)

Benediktinerkloster, Musikbibliothek [Ben. 13]
CH 8840, Einsiedeln   Tel: (055) 6 14 31
Hours: by appointment only.
Founded in about 950, this library has a total collection of 110,000 volumes, 1200 manuscripts, and 1000 *incunabula.*

Lausanne (Vaud)

Bibliothèque Cantonale et Universitaire [Ben. 20]
6 place de la Riponne, CH 1005

Conservatoire de Musique, Bibliothèque [Ben. 21]
6 rue du Midi, CH 1000   Tel: (021) 22 26 08
Hours: Monday, Wednesday, Friday, 4:00 PM to 6:00 PM. Closed school holidays.

Luzern (Lucerne)

Zentralbibliothek [Ben. 25]
10 Sempacherstrasse

Neuchâtel (Neuenberg)

Bibliothèque Publique de la Ville [Ben. 27]
3 place Numa-Droz   Tel: (038) 5 13 58
An extensive collection with considerable material on Rousseau, including autographs and manuscripts; also eighteenth-century Italian manuscripts of operas and symphonies.

St. Gallen (St. Gall)

Stadtbibliothek (Vadiana) [Ben. 29]
22 Notkerstrasse

Stiftsbibliothek St. Gallen [Ben. 30]
6 Klosterhof   Tel: (071) 22 57 19
Hours: May to October, Monday to Saturday 9:00 AM to noon; 2:00 PM to 5:00
     PM; Sunday 10:30 AM to noon (June through August, also 2:00 PM to 4:00
     PM.) November to April, Monday 9:00 AM to noon; Tuesday to Saturday
     9:00 AM to noon and 2:00 PM to 4:00 PM.
Many ninth- to eighteenth-century liturgical manuscripts are in this famous
library, formerly a Benedictine abbey.

Neues Museum (Historische Abteilung) Instrumenten Sammlung
50 Museumstrasse   Tel: (071) 24 78 32
Hours: April to October, Tuesday to Saturday 10:00 AM to noon; 2:00 PM to 5:00
     PM; Sunday 10:00 AM to noon; 2:00 PM to 4:00 PM. November to March,
     Tuesday to Sunday 10:00 AM to noon; 2:00 PM to 4:00 PM. (Wednesday,
     Saturday afternoons, and all day Sunday free.)

Zofingen (Aargau)

Stadtbibliothek [Ben. 38]
18 Obere Grabenstrasse
This library has a collection of Wagner and Schumann autographs, as well as
correspondence of several other musicians and conductors.

See also *The Swiss Music Library* (USA)
444 Madison Avenue, New York, N.Y. 10022
Marguerite Staehelin, the Director, commutes between this address and her
address in Basel, 38 Weiherweg, 4000 Basel.

Musical Landmarks

Lucerne

Richard Wagner Museum
Triebschen 6000   Tel: (041) 44 23 70
Hours: Monday to Saturday, 9:00 AM to noon; 2:00 PM to 6:00 PM; Sunday, 10:30
     AM to noon and 2:00 PM to 5:00 PM. From October 15 to April 15, closed on
     Monday, Wednesday, and Friday. (This information provided on our
     questionnaire. At Museum, literature distributed indicates that the Mu-
     seum is closed during this period on Tuesday, Thursday, and Saturday
     during those months. Best to check by calling Tourist Office, (041) 2 52 22
     in Lucerne.)
Triebschen was Wagner's home from 1866 to 1872, while he completed *Die*

Meistersinger, Siegfried, and *Götterdämmerung.* The house stands in the center of a charming park that borders on Lake Lucerne. The Museum, opened in 1933, contains autographs of the *Siegfried Idyll* and the "Schusterlied" (Cobbler's Song) from *Die Meistersinger.* Other objects of interest include Wagner's death mask, several portraits of him, etchings, busts, scores, letters, photographs, and the Érard grand piano that accompanied the composer to Venice, Paris, Vienna, Munich, Triebschen, and Bayreuth.

The *Siegfried Idyll* was written here and performed for the first time on Christmas morning 1870 in the "Treppenhaus" (the landing on the stairs) in honor of Cosima's birthday.

On the second floor (first floor in Swiss parlance) you will find a collection of old instruments, both Western and non-Western.

Conservatories and Schools

In addition to the conservatories or universities mentioned below, the following cities have established conservatories: Biel, La Chaux-de-fonds, Fribourg, Lausanne, Neuchâtel, Sion, Winterthur. For the less advanced student, there are schools of music in Baden, Chur, Lausanne, Lucerne, Schaffhausen, Vevey.

Lucerne (Luzern)

Konservatorium Luzern
93 Dreilindenstrasse
Note: There are housing provisions for students here in regular dormitories.

Master Classes at Konzervatorium Luzern
(see address above)
In association with the Conservatory, master courses in piano, violin, cello, chamber music, and singing are held during the Festival (see below). These courses are open to artists and students of sufficiently high standard to pursue their studies successfully under one of the masters. Fees must be paid no later than the start of the course. Participants may attend the final rehearsal of specific symphony concerts.

Applications and inquiries should be made to above address. Number of active participants is limited; auditors will be accepted for entire period of course only. Recent faculty included Mieczyslaw Horoszowski, piano; Wolfgang Schneiderhan, violin.

Lausanne

University of Lausanne
4 place de la Cathédrale
The University offers an exchange scholarship to an American student with an A.B. and an adequate knowledge of French. Write Institute of International Education, 809 United Nations Plaza, New York, N.Y. 10017.

Neuchâtel

University of Neuchâtel
26 avenue du 1er-Mars
The University offers four exchange scholarships to students from countries offering the same kind of scholarships to their students. The United States is one of them. Students must have their A.B. and an adequate knowledge of French. Write Institute of International Education, 809 United Nations Plaza, New York, N.Y. 10017.

Courses at all of these schools are given in the original language, i.e., French or German. Therefore, a good working knowledge of either French or German is necessary.

Musical Organizations

Lausanne

Association des agents de spectacle et concerts en Suisse
2 bis Grand-Pont
This organization is a good source of information on concerts, master classes, festivals, etc., in Switzerland.

Three organizations, the Internationale Gesellschaft für neue Musik (International Society for Contemporary Music), the Jeunesses Musicales de Suisse, and the Swiss Music Council are all located at 11 bis avenue du Gramont, Lausanne.

Neuchâtel

Conférence des Directeurs de conservatoires Suisses
Faubourg de l'Hôpital

SYMPHONY ORCHESTRAS

Lausanne

Orchestre de Chambre de Lausanne
2 bis Grand-Pont

Radio Suisse Romande
Maison de la Radio   Tel: (021) 21 71 11

Lucerne

Allgemeine Musikgesellschaft Luzern
50 Dreilindenstrasse   Tel: (041) 44 19 28

Lugano

Orchestra della Radio Svizzera Italiana
6903 Lugano   Tel: (09) 3 30 21

St. Gallen

Konzertverein der Stadt St. Gallen
40 Tannenstrasse   Tel: (071) 24 25 83

The Business of Music

CONCERT MANAGERS

Lausanne

International Booking Agency
    8 Victor Ruffy   Tel: (021) 23 96 78

Robert Schlaepfer & Jean Couroyer Agence d'Orchestres & de Spectacles
    36 rue St. Martin   Tel: (021) 23 28 87

Lucerne

M.v. Kaenel
    c/o Hug & Co., 52–56 Hertensteinstrasse

Festivals

Ascona

Festival of Music
Mailing Address: Festival of Music, 6612 Ascona.
Dates: August to October.
Classical music.

Berne

Berne Art Weeks
Mailing Address: Official Tourist Office and Convention Bureau of the city of
  Berne, 20 Bundesgasse, CH-3011 Berne   Tel: (031) 22 39 51
Dates: end of May to end of June.
Box office for Stadttheater:
Advance bookings: written requests for reserved seats for all performances in
  Stadttheater can be made in advance, except for the middle and side of the
  gallery and the first, second, and third rows center of the upper gallery.
  Tickets can be reserved only until thirty minutes before the start of the
  program for people from outside Berne. Residents of Berne have to collect
  their tickets by 12:30 PM on the day of the performance; otherwise the seats
  can be redistributed.
Advance sales: sale of tickets for individual performances starts five days before
  presentation (inclusive) and can also be ordered by telephone from that
  date with a call to the advance booking office, 3 Predigergasse. It is open
  10:00 AM to 12:30 PM and 3:00 PM to 6:45 PM weekdays, and 10:00 AM to
  12:30 PM Sunday. The ticket office is also open an hour before the start of
  performances. Concessionary theater privileges do not apply except for gift
  coupons, subscription tickets, and franc coupons from the Berner Theater-
  verein.
Hours: This office is open Monday to Friday 8:00 AM to noon and 2:00 PM to 6:00
  PM; Saturday 8:00 AM to noon.
Operas, concerts, ballet, plays, art exhibits.
  Berne Art Weeks have replaced the original Opera Weeks of the Municipal
Theater and have been taking place since June 1970. Participating institutes
(including guest companies) present to the public special performances which
are typical of their work. Under the theme, "Berne Art Weeks," they offer not so
much the program of a festival, but rather highlight the cultural life of Berne in
June. Performances are given in the Stadttheater Bern, Berner Münster, Casino
Bern, and Radio DRS Studio Bern. For box office information concerning the
latter three, consult the Official Tourist Office and Convention Bureau of Berne
(see address and telephone number above).

Engadine

Engadiner Konzert-Wochen—Internationale Kammermusikfestspiele
Büro des Oberengadiner Kurvereins (opposite Hotel Bernina)
Samedan
Dates: mid-July to mid-August.
Box Office: in July and August, Monday to Friday 4:30 PM to 6:30 PM.
Chamber music concerts.

Gstaad

Yehudi Menuhin Festival
Mailing Address: Verkehrsbüro, 3780 Gstaad, Berner Oberland
Dates: early August to early September (ten to fifteen concerts)
Box Office: same address as above. Tickets may be returned until 4:00 PM of day
   of performance. Concerts begin at 8:30 PM. Single tickets from a subscrip-
   tion may not be refunded or exchanged.
Seating Capacity: 800 in church, where concerts are given.
Chamber concerts and solo recitals.

Herriberg

Ander Foldes Festival
Mailing Address: Ander Foldes Festival, 8704 Herriberg/ZH
Dates: June 10 to July 1.
Chamber music.

Interlaken

Interlaken Festival Weeks
Mailing Address: Sekretariat der Mozart-Woche Interlaken, Kursaal, Interla-
   ken   Tel: (036) 22 17 13
Dates: two weeks at the end of June and beginning of July.
Box Office: for the Festival, opens at the end of May.
Symphony concerts, opera, ballet, opera ball.
   The Gesellschaft der Freunde der Interlakner Musikfestwochen is a spon-
soring group of this festival. Performances take place in Casino-Kursaal.

Lausanne

Lausanne International Festival
Théâtre Municipal de Lausanne, Case Postale 1373, 1002 Lausanne
Dates: end of April to end of June.

Orchestral and choral concerts, recitals, operas, ballets.

Festival of Italian Opera
(Same address as above)
Dates: October.

The International Youth Orchestra Festival
Mailing Address: Festival international d'orchestres des jeunes, Case Postale 572, 1002 Lausanne Tel: (021) 27 73 21
Dates: two weeks at the end of July and the beginning of August.
Box Office: bookings can be made starting at the beginning of July at the Théâtre Municipal de Lausanne. The office is open from 10:00 AM to 12:30 PM and from 1:30 PM to 6:30 PM. Seats can be reserved in advance by writing or telephoning. In that case, the total amount must be paid by money order to Caisse du Théâtre Municipal, Lausanne, at least one week before the beginning of the festival.
Concerts, ballet.
This festival presents concerts by youth orchestras and ensembles from all over the world. The best players form an International Festival Youth Orchestra for the final concert under an outstanding guest conductor. Concerts take place in the Théâtre de Beaulieu. Ballet is also presented, including performances by guest companies, in the Théâtre Municipal. Some of the youth orchestras which play in this festival also perform other concerts in Switzerland at different towns throughout the country.

Lucerne

Lucerne International Festival of Music (IMF) or Internationale Musikfestwochen
Mailing Address: 4 Schweizerhofquai, 6002 Lucerne
Dates: from middle of August to early September (three and a half weeks).
Box Office: Kunsthaus (Concert Hall).
Advance Sale: Lucerne International Festival of Music Advance Booking Department, P.O. Box 6002, Lucerne.
Hours: weekdays, 10:00 AM to noon and 4:00 PM to 6:00 PM; Saturday, 10:00 AM to noon only; these hours are from mid-July to end of Festival; additional hours during Festival, Saturday and Sunday, 4:00 PM to 5:00 PM (subject to change). No standing room.
Seating Capacity: 1842.
Dress: in accordance with formal character of festival. At symphony concerts, gentlemen usually wear dark suits.
Housing Information: Lucerne Hotel Association, 5 Lidostrasse, Lucerne.

Symphonic and choral concerts, chamber music, serenades, recitals, Musica Nova, master courses, theatrical events, exhibitions.

Meiringen

Musikfestwochen Meiringen
Mailing Address: Verkehrsbüro Meiringen, 3860 Meiringen   Tel: (036) 72 21 31
Dates: early July.
Chamber orchestras and ensembles.
This festival includes six concerts in the church at Meiringen. It is sponsored by the Gesellschaft der Freunde der Interlakner Festwoche.

Montreux

International Jazz Festival
Mailing Address: International Jazz Festival, P.O. Box 97, 1820 Montreux

European Jazz Orchestra Competition
Sponsor: European Broadcasting Union.

Montreux-Vevey

Montreux-Vevey Festival (September Musical)
Mailing Address: 42 Grand'rue CH-1820, Montreux.
Dates: end of August (or beginning of September) to early October. Concerts held in various halls, churches, castles.
Seating Capacity: 500 to 1,500 depending on hall.
Box Office: Tourist Office/Festival de Musique (same as mail address). For Vevey: ADIVE (Office of Tourism), place de la Gare, also Foetisch Frères S.A., 15 rue des Deux-Marches.
Housing Information: Tourist Office (address above).

Sion, Valais

Festival Tibor Varga (Association du Festival Tibor Varga)
Mailing Address: Case Postale No. 428, 1950 Sion VS/Suisse. 10 rue de la Dixence, 1950 Sion (Public Entrance)
Dates: usually at end of July.
Box Office: Hallenbarter & Cie, rue Remparts, 1950 Sion.   Tel: (027) 2 10 63
Hours: weekdays 8:00 AM to noon, 1:30 PM to 6:30 PM.
Authorized Ticket Agency: Touralp SA, 25 avenue de la Gare, 1950 Sion.

Housing Information: Office du Tourisme de Sion, 6 rue de Lausanne, 1950 Sion, Valais.   Tel: (027) 2 28 98

Valais

Festival de Ribaupierre—Semaines Musicales du Valais

Mailing Address: Concerts d'Evolène-Les Haudères: Festival de Ribaupierre, 1961 Les Haudères, Valais, Switzerland
Dates: end of July to end of August.
Primarily chamber music concerts (piano and violin sonatas).

Zurich

Internationale Juni-Festwochen (Zurich International June Festival)

c/o Verkehrsverein, Zürich, Postfach 8023
Dates: June each year.
Box Offices: Opera House (see address above); also Concert Hall (Tonhalle-Gesellschaft); and Zürcher Kammerorchester (55 Sekretariat Kreuzstrasse)
Hours: 10:00 AM to 7:00 PM weekdays; Sunday, 10:00 AM to noon and 3:00 PM to 5:00 PM as well as one hour before beginning of performances. For Concert Hall: 9:00 AM to 12:30 PM and 3:00 PM to 6:00 PM as well as one hour before performances. Closed Saturday and Sunday afternoons. For Zürcher Kammerorchester: 9:00 AM to noon, 3:00 PM to 6:00 PM as well as one hour before performances. Closed Saturday afternoon and Sunday. Operas and plays begin at 8:00 PM; concerts at 8:15 PM.
Ballet, opera, concerts, plays, exhibitions of modern and contemporary art.

Authorized Ticket Agencies:
Kuoni Travel Agency
7 Bahnhofplatz
Hours: 8:30 AM to 5:30 PM daily; Saturday 8:30 AM to noon.
Opera, theater, concerts.

Hug & Co.
28 Limmatquai
Concerts.

Pianohaus Jecklin
Pfauen
Concerts.

Housing Information: Verkehrsverein Zürich, 15 Bahnhofplatz.

Competitions

Baden

International Komponisten Wettbewerb (International Composers' Contest)
Stiftung Alte Kirche Boswil, 6 Bruggerstrasse, CH 5400 Baden
Dates: about last week in April.
Deadline: January 15; no age limit.

Geneva

Concours international d'Exécution musicale (International Competition for Musical Performance)
Palais Eynard, CH 1204
Dates: end of September to beginning of October.
Awards: total of Sfr 64,000.
Deadline: July 1. Women singers 20 to 30 years old; men singers 22 to 32; instrumentalists 15 to 30.
This competition is usually held annually. The categories change. For example, in 1970: piano, voice, violin, organ, and saxophone; in 1971: voice, piano, cello, oboe, and French horn; in 1972: voice, piano, viola, clarinet, and percussion.

Concours international de Composition Opéra et Ballet (Opera and Ballet International Composition Competition)
Maison de la Radio, 66 boulevard Carl Vogt
Dates: not given.
Awards: first prize of Sfr 12,000 and possible production by the Grand Theater of Geneva.
Deadline: September 1; no age limits.
This contest is held every two years. Categories alternate between opera and ballet. In 1971, opera; in 1973, ballet.

Secrétariat du Prix de Composition Musicale Reine Marie-José (Queen Marie-José Prize for Musical Composition)
CH-1249 Merlinge-Gy
Dates: not given.
Awards: one prize of Sfr 10,000; performance of work.
Deadline: for submission of manuscripts, usually May 31; no age limits.
This competition is also biennial. The type of composition changes; in 1972 it was chamber music, a composition for three to eight performers, of ten to thirty minutes' duration. Instruments to be used are prescribed.

Lucerne

Clara Haskil Competition

Although this contest has not been held since 1969, information about it can be obtained by interested pianists from Hanny Kurzmeyer, Sekretariat, Concours Clara Haskil, Konservatorium, 82 Dreilindenstrasse, 6000 Lucerne.

Montreux

International Flute Contest

Secrétariat General, Concours International de Flûte de Montreux
42 Grande-Rue
Dates: end of August or beginning of September to beginning of October.
Awards: three prizes totaling Sfr 5,000. A flute for each winner. Public performances on radio and in concert.
Deadline: about July 10; flutists under 30 are eligible, regardless of nationality.
This competition is held annually.

Sion (Valais)

Tibor Varga Violin Competition (Festival de Musique)

Casa Postale 428, CH-1950 Sion (Valais)
Dates: not given.
Awards: Sfr 5,000; 7 other prizes totaling Sfr 8,000.
Deadline: June 1; 15 to 35 years of age.
This contest is held annually. In addition, for the past eight years, master courses (cours d'interprétation or Meisterkurse) are given at the same time as the festival (see above). Soloists, both professional and amateur, as well as auditors may participate in these courses. In 1972, special courses for violinists, clarinetists, pianists, and trumpeters were given. The categories change yearly.

Periodicals

Acta Musicologica

Bärenreiter-Verlag, 15 Neuweileirstrasse, 4000 Basel 15
Quarterly to members
Published by the International Musicological Society under the auspices of the International Music Council with the assistance of UNESCO. Contains articles written in French, German, English, and occasionally Italian.

Arts et Musique (Official organ of the Jeunesses Musicales of Switzerland)
66 boulevard Carl Vogt, 1211 Geneva 8
Monthly

Bulletin de l'Association Suisse des Chasseurs de Sons
Case Postale 2211, 3000 Bern

Conservatoire de Musique de Genève, Bulletin
Conservatoire de Musique, place Neuve, 1204 Geneva
10 issues yearly

Dissonanz (Organ of the Organization of Music Students)
6 Florhofgasse, 8001 Zürich

Eidgenössisches Sängerblatt (Bulletin of the Confederation of Choral Societies)
2 Pfaffensteinstrasse, 8122 Pfaffhausen
Monthly

Eidgenössische Sängerzeitung (Swiss Singers' Review)
2 Pfaffensteinstrasse, 8122 Pfaffhausen
Bimonthly

Der Evangelische Kirchenchor (Bulletin of the Swiss Church Choral Societies)
Zwingli-Verlag, Postfach 8021, Zürich
Bimonthly

Festivals
European Association of Music Festivals, 122 rue de Lausanne, Geneva
Annually

Feuilles Musicales
Postfach 30, Lausanne 19

Hillbilly
P.O. Box 1, CH-4000, Basel 4
Quarterly

International Inventory of Musical Sources (International Musicological Society & International Association of Music Libraries)

Bärenreiter-Verlag, 15 Neuweilerstrasse, 4000 Basel

Jazz-Rhythm and Blues (Text in English, French, and German)
Postfach 350, 8050 Zürich
Monthly
U.S. Subscriptions: Hans M. Zell, 11 Waverly Place, New York, N.Y. 10003

Kirchensänger (Newsletter of Catholic Church Choruses)
Paulus Verlag GmbH, 41 Pilatusstrasse, 6000 Lucerne
Four to six times yearly

Musik und Gottesdienst (Journal of Protestant Church Music)
Zwingli-Verlag, 17 Cramerstrasse, Postfach 8021, 8004 Zürich
Bimonthly

Revue Musicale de Suisse Romande (This publication now includes *Feuilles Musicales, Courrier Suisse du Disque, Revue Romande de Musique, Organe des Jeunesses Musicales de Suisse.*)
1000 Lausanne
Quarterly

Schweizer Musikerblatt
35 Thalacker, Zürich 1
Monthly

Schweizerische Blasmusikzeitung (Swiss Bulletin of Woodwind Music)
7 Dunanstrasse, 3006 Bern
Twice monthly

Schweizerische Musikforschende Gesellschaft Mitteilungsblatt
(Swiss Music Research)
25 Passangstrasse, Basel

Schweizer Musiker-Revue
3142 Bahnpostfach, Zürich
Monthly

Schweizerische Musikzeitung (Swiss Musical Review)
Verlag Hug & Co., 8022 Zürich
Bimonthly

Schweizerische Zeitschrift für Musikhandel und Industrie
(Text in French and German)

Buchdruckerei K.J. Wyss Erben AG, 17 Effingerstrasse, Bern
Eight times yearly

Singt und Spielt

Gebrüder Hug & Co., 29 Dorflistrasse, Zürich 57

La Tribune de l'Orgue

12 avenue Tivoli, 1007 Lausanne
Five times yearly

Appendix

Several organizations with offices in New York City and others with offices abroad can be of service to those intending to spend several months or a year studying in Europe. They include the following:

Institute of International Education
809 United Nations Plaza, New York, N.Y. 10017   Tel: (212) 883-8200

Council on International Educational Exchange'
777 United Nations Plaza, New York, N.Y. 10017   Tel: (212) 661-0310
(Paris address of the CIEE: 49 rue Pierre Charron, Paris VIII)

Institute for American Universities (under the suspices of)
University of Aix-Marseille, 27 place de l'Université, 13, Aix-en-Provence, France.

Some organizations can provide assistance in locating employment abroad. These include:

International School Services, Educational Staffing Program
392 Fifth Avenue, New York, N.Y. 10018

American Association of Colleges for Teacher Education
Associate Secretary for International Relations
One Dupont Circle, Suite 610, Washington, D.C. 20036

U.S. Government, Committee on International Exchange of Persons
Senior Fulbright-Hays Program
2101 Constitution Avenue, N.W., Washington, D.C. 20418

Recruitment and Source Development Staff, Office of Personnel and Training
U.S. Information Agency, Washington, D.C. 20547

Finally, two additional organizations that can help you if you intend to stay abroad for a considerable length of time:

Sabbatical Year in Europe
265 Maple Avenue, Morton, Pa. 19070

This organization provides information on special rates for sabbatical flights, establishes contacts with Europeans who are willing to advise you on your sabbatical, and helps make available an exchange of apartments for its members.

Vacation Exchange Club
663 Fifth Avenue, New York, N.Y. 10036.
This group helps to arrange an exchange of homes or apartments for those who need it.

It is advisable when writing to any of these organizations to state your reasons for going abroad and to ask for practical as well as professional advice for your visit. In the United States, send along a stamped, self-addressed envelope. When writing to foreign organizations, send an International Reply Coupon, available at most local post offices. This added courtesy should assure you a more prompt reply.

For additional information on living in various countries of Europe during a sabbatical year, consult *Shoestring Sabbatical*, edited by Harold E. Taussig (Philadelphia, Pa.: Westminster Press, 1971).

Reference Books for the Student or Scholar Going Abroad

European Library Directory: A Geographical and Bibliographical Guide. Richard C. Lewanski, Florence: Olschki, 1968.
Fellowship Guide for Western Europe, published by the Council of European Studies, 213 Social Sciences Building, University of Pittsburgh, Pittsburgh, Pa. 15213
    The *Fellowship Guide* is intended for American graduate students, faculty, and researchers in the social sciences and humanities who need funds for study or research in Western Europe. Included is information about those fellowships that permit an extended stay abroad (usually one academic year), either in residence at a specific foreign university or for independent research.
Guide to Study in Europe. Shirley Herman. New York: Four Winds Press. 1969.

Handbook on International Study for U.S. Nationals. New York: Institute of International Education.

International Library Directory: A World Directory of Libraries, 3rd ed. A. P. Wales. London: The A. P. Wales Organization, 1969-70.

Performing Arts Libraries and Museums of the World. André Veinstein, Paris: Editions du CNRS, 1967.

Study Abroad. Paris: United Nations, Educational, Scientific and Cultural Organization, 1969.

Subject Collections in European Libraries: A Directory and Bibliographical Guide. Richard C. Lewanski. New York: Bowker, 1965.

Youth Travel Abroad: What to Know Before You Go. This pamphlet is issued by the State Department and is designed to help young Americans abroad. It is available for 20 cents from the U.S. Government Printing Office, Washington, D.C. 20402.

Additional Information for Student Travelers

A *Student Travelpack* put together by the Council on International Educational Exchange includes information on discounts available to students, intra-European charter flights, youth fares, student tours, etc. It can be obtained free from the Council at 777 United Nations Plaza, New York, N.Y. 10017

The Council also issues to eligible students, at a cost of $2.00, the *International Student Identity Card* (for college undergraduates and graduate students) and the *International Scholar Identity Card* (for high school and other nonuniversity students). These are accepted throughout Western Europe for discounts on intra-European air, train, and bus travel, low-cost tours, student lodgings, and meals in student restaurants. Several cities will give student rates for concerts and opera performances if one presents an I.S.I.D. card, although this does not apply to all theaters in those cities. Museums often give discounts too. The cards are valid from October 1 of one year to December 31 of the following year.

The Student Air Travel Association

British Student Travel Centre, Suite 1602, 80 Fifth Avenue, New York, N.Y. 10011   Tel: (212) 243-9114

This organization operates student charter flights. For information, write to the above address.

International Student Exchange

Europa House, University of Illinois, 802 West Oregon, Urbana, Ill. 61801
                                                     Tel: (217) 344-5863

This organization arranges study trips in Europe.

Internationaler Jugendaustausch—und Besucherdienst
Lennestrasse 1, D 53 Bonn, Germany

This organization provides information about vacation language courses which combine language instruction and tours of Germany.

Council on Intercultural Relations
3 South Prospect Avenue, Park Ridge, Ill. 60068
Director: Mr. Paul F. Koutny
Austrian Branch: Bindergasse 5-9, A-1090 Vienna IX, Austria   Tel: 34 33 60

This organization sponsors the Undergraduate Program at the Vienna International Music Center, which offers American college students a music study program for a semester or the entire year. The Council also makes special arrangements for faculty on sabbatical to do research in Vienna. In addition, it co-sponsors with the American Choral Directors Association the Vienna Symposium for American Choral Directors (held in June and August). For further information, write to above addresses.

The Institute of European Studies
The John Hancock Center, 875 North Michigan Avenue, Chicago, Ill. 60611
Tel: (312) 944-1750

The Institute offers American college students a variety of programs in six European cities: Durham, Freiburg, Madrid, Nantes, Paris, and Vienna. The Institute offers its own courses taught in many fields by European professors, but it also encourages students to take regular European university courses for which they have satisfactory preparation. Only the Vienna and Nantes programs offer courses in music. The Extension Division of the Institute provides services for a complete range of tours, workshops, and professional programs for the American musician—students and professionals alike. In addition, the Institute sponsors music festivals from time to time. For complete information, write to the above address.

International Institute for Humanistic Studies
3718 Dumbarton Street, Houston, Tex. 77025

This institute sponsors master courses in music in Vienna and Salzburg from the end of May through the end of June. The Piano Master Course was given in 1973 by Paul Badura-Skoda, Jorge Demus, Viola Thern, and Eva Badura-Skoda; the faculty of the Seminar in Baroque Performance Practices included Nikolaus Harnoncourt, Alice Harnoncourt, Christoph Wolff, and Herbert Tachezi.

Certificates of attendance will be awarded all persons successfully participating in the piano course and performance practices seminar. A limited number of scholarships is available. Undergraduate and graduate students are eligible. Pianists who wish to apply for a scholarship must send a tape by April 1. For further information, write to the above address.

International Postal Abbreviations for European Countries (For Intra-European Mail Only)

These abbreviations are to be used *only* when writing from one European country to another. For example, when writing to the Palais des Beaux-Arts in Brussels from Paris, the address of the Palais should be: 23 rue Ravenstein, B-1000 Bruxelles. (The "B" stands for Belgium.) When writing to the Palais from Brussels or anywhere else in Belgium, the address is simply 23 rue Ravenstein, 1000 Bruxelles. (The "B" is unnecessary within the country.) However, when writing from the United States to Belgium, be sure that the address has Belgium *as well as* 1000 Bruxelles indicated on the envelope.

Austria = A
Belgium = B
Denmark = DK
Finland = SF
France = F
Germany = D
Great Britain = GB
Italy = I
Netherlands = NL
Norway = N
Sweden = S
Switzerland = CH

Index

Index